All Saints Day

Sean Patrick Doles

New Orleans Stories
New Orleans/Austin

PRINTED IN THE UNITED STATES OF AMERICA

Visit our website at www.neworleansstories.com.

New Orleans Stories and its logo, the letters N and O stacked
vertically, are trademarks of New Orleans Stories. "Baghead"
photograph © David Rae Morris.

New Orleans Stories
7301 Burnet Rd., Ste. 102, PMB 107
Austin, TX 78757

First New Orleans Stories paperback printing: August, 2005
Library of Congress Control Number: 2005905837

ISBN 978-0-9758996-1-8

1 3 5 7 9 10 8 6 4 2

*"There is only one religion,
though there are a hundred versions of it."*

George Bernard Shaw

For Hap Glaudi, Buddy D, Mr. Finks,
and all the patient, dedicated
New Orleans Saints fans
across the globe.

Prologue

Once upon a time...

Announcer: We welcome you back to the New Orleans Saints Radio Network. This is Tim Anderson here with former LSU and Saints legend CoCo Pichon in the Louisiana Superdome. Only six seconds remain in what has been the most entertaining game in recent memory, as the Saints have come storming back from a 17-point, fourth-quarter deficit against the Carolina Panthers to take a 28-24 lead on a 3-yard touchdown pass from Robbie Gauthier to Jordash Jones.

CoCo: The Saints musta' jus' been playin' possum for the first three quarters, because they been hotter than fish grease since about the 10-minute mark.

Anderson: Yes, CoCo, at 0-and-7 and down by three scores, the Saints looked dead to rights, as did their prospects for this season. But we've seen a resurrection of sorts here in the last few minutes.

CoCo: All they gotta' do now is squib this kickoff and make a tackle, and they can record their first "W" of the season.

Anderson: That shouldn't be a problem, as kicker Oleg Adamowicz prepares to tee it up. In the background, you can still hear the crowd chanting "GO-SHAY GO-SHAY", hailing their much-maligned quarterback, who has gone 10 of 14 for 174 yards and three touchdowns over the last 8:43 of the game.

CoCo: The crowd's about to blow the lid off this place. It may be the loudest I've heard them all season. Course, they ain't had much to cheer about lately. But if the Saints pull this one out, I'm afraid to see what the fans will do next. We'll have to barricade Bourbon Street.

Anderson: The usually stoic Adamowicz is even getting into the act, egging on the crowd. The former European soccer star finally seems to be adjusting to American football.

CoCo: Tim, you know I ain't much for squib kicks. Seems like these days more crazy things happen off the squib than a deep kick. But I gotta' say, with a 4-point lead and six ticks left, in this case it seems like the right play.

Anderson: Well, we won't prolong the suspense any further, as Adamowicz addresses the ball. The Saints are going left to right on your radio dial, and they're...

CoCo: What the hell?

Anderson: Oh, it's not a squib. Adamowicz kicks it deep, and it'll be taken at the 2-yard line by Willie Coleman, who follows his blockers along the right hash to the 10, 15, cuts to the sideline, surrounded by Saints, he stops... turns...throws the ball across the field and...

CoCo: Uh-oh!

Anderson: He's got Chuckie Winter wide open at the 15.

CoCo: Uh-oh! This is like a flashback to the Music City Miracle.

Anderson: Winter races up the sideline... 30... 40...50. There's only one man to beat.

CoCo: Lord have mercy.

Anderson: Oleg has the angle on him. All he has to do is push Winter out of bounds, and the game is over. Winter's at the 40...30...20.

CoCo: Looks like Oleg's gonna' catch him. He's going to...

Anderson: OUCH! Adamowicz is blindsided at the 10-yard line with a bone-crushing block, and Winter is going to go in for the score.

CoCo: Oh my God!

Anderson: Time has expired. There are no penalty flags. The Panthers have won the game, apparently, and the crowd is showering the referees with boos.

CoCo: They wanted a clipping penalty, but the hit on Adamowicz was clean.

Anderson: The Saints are wandering around

the field, their helmets off, stunned, as the Panthers celebrate in the end zone. Adamowicz is still sprawled on the turf at the 10-yard line.

CoCo: He ain't movin', Tim. I think he got knocked into next week on that hit.

Anderson: The officiating staff has beaten a hasty retreat into the tunnel, and now the crowd's ire has turned to the home team, who are making their way off the field.

CoCo: Oh man, this is gettin' ugly.

Anderson: The boos continue, as angry fans have begun pelting the Saints' players with plastic beer bottles and cups.

CoCo: All that Dome foam goin' to waste. They really need to cut off beer sales at halftime.

Anderson: Several of the Saints are now challenging fans in the stands, but security is doing their best to herd the team into the tunnel, as liquids continue to rain down on them, seemingly from every corner of the stadium. And from the sound of it, the boos are growing louder.

CoCo: There ain't nobody left on the field to boo, unless you want to count Oleg and the medical staff who are workin' on him.

Anderson: And it does appear to be a rather serious situation, as the Saints' trainers have signaled for a neck brace and back board.

CoCo: Looks like they got his helmet off and they're trying to...oh my goodness, they're bringin' out them air-hockey lookin' paddles.

Anderson: Without a doubt, this has certainly taken a turn for the worse. One of the Saints' staff is now holding up a towel as if to shield the activity from view.

CoCo: Looks like now the fans have decided to take their anger out on the poor kicker.

Anderson: That does appear to be the case.

CoCo: Tim, this is absolutely disgusting. These fans are showing no class whatsoever.

Anderson: It's especially disconcerting in light of what appears to be a grave situation.

CoCo: And besides, like my Mama always said, you don't kick a man when he's down... 'cause he might get up.

Anderson: CoCo, I think you're right and... wow, that beer bottle must have flown 50 yards in the air before it hit the assistant trainer in the back of the head. He looks a little woozy.

CoCo: He ain't woozy. He's going down.

Anderson: Yes, yes, he is. So now we have two men down, although it looks like the crisis with Adamowicz has passed, and they're loading him onto the medical cart. Well, I guess in that respect, we can breathe a sigh of relief.

CoCo: This is an embarrassment. An embarrassment to the team, to the league, to the city of New Orleans, and to the people of Louisiana.

Anderson: In an organization that's had more than its share of lows, this ugly episode may well be the lowest.

Week 9 (bye week)
Saints' Record: 0 wins, 8 losses

"The Pope wants to do *what*?"

Archbishop Frances Boudreaux shouted into the phone as though he were speaking to someone across the Atlantic Ocean, when, in reality, the person on the other end of the line was sitting just down the hall, inside the living quarters at the Archdiocese of New Orleans main offices.

"The *Saints*? I'm sorry, are you referring to the cemeteries, St. Louis No. 1 and No. 2? They are among the most popular tourist attractions in the city. Are you saying His Holiness would like to take a tour? We can certainly arrange that."

Although language had posed only a minimal barrier between Boudreaux and Pope Pius XIII's cadre of handlers in the two days since their arrival, these minor miscommunications were still inevitable. The aging Archbishop with the distinct Cajun accent chuckled at the request. Then he frowned upon hearing the response.

"Wait a second. You're referring to the *football team*? You're saying that the Pope would like to have an audience with the New Orleans Saints football team? He does understand that this is American football, not soccer, right?"

Boudreaux shook his head and then gazed down at his thick-soled black oxfords, simultaneously rubbing his forehead with his free hand.

"Well, no, no, it's not that. It's just, well...it's just that they're *not very good*. To be frank, they're terrible. I'm a little worried about how this might reflect on the church and...yes, yes sir. I understand. Certainly. Yes, I'll call the team right away."

Boudreaux's concern was justifiable from a number of standpoints, especially that there might be better uses of the Holy Father's time. By all estimations, given his failing health, this would likely mark his last trip to New Orleans.

In recent weeks, the 94-year-old Pope had taken to blessing everything in sight. One day earlier, during mass at the Superdome with a crowd of 100,000 looking on, he had seen fit to bless a Zapp's Cajun-Crawtator chip supposedly bearing the likeness of the Virgin Mary. Needless to say, though the Pope remained infallible, his decisions were still open to questioning.

But in light of the Pope's gracious agreement to visit and give the financially strapped Archdiocese a much-needed shot in the arm, Boudreaux was obliged to acquiesce. Resigned to the task, he hung up the phone and reported the news to his trusted assistant, Monsignor Fitzpatrick.

"The *Saints*?" Fitzpatrick said, also incredulous. "Why on earth would the Pope want to have a private audience with the Saints?"

Boudreaux shrugged. "He says they do the Lord's work...and that this city needs all the help it can get. Get me the phone number of Ron Beauchamp."

***

"The Pope wants to do *what*?" Coach Jake "The Anvil" Radke snapped in his sharp Chicago accent, having been rousted from his mid-morning meditative ritual by the ringing phone.

The meditation, to be fair, had nothing to do with New Age mysticism or Eastern religion. Rather, it consisted of Radke's staring at the bottom drawer of his desk, locked in a battle with his conscience to decide whether or not to uncork the magical elixir inside: a bottle of 12-year-old Jack Daniel's Special Reserve.

In the end, despite the struggle between his head and his heart, the gnawing ache in his gut would always win out, and Radke would find some small measure of relief from the torment of coaching one of the most hapless franchises in the history of the National Football League.

In this age of instant gratification, few fans would recall that the vaunted Pittsburgh Steelers had endured a staggering 40 years of futility before striking gold in the 1974 Super Bowl under the leadership of Terry Bradshaw, himself a Louisiana boy from Ruston. Or the Cincinnati Bengals, who, despite reaching two Super Bowls during the 1980s, had since gone 20 straight seasons without a winning record. Or the Seattle Seahawks, who had gone more than two decades without winning a playoff game.

No, for long-suffering fans of the New Orleans Saints, having tasted only sorrow and disappointment, heartbreak and bitterness, perspective such as this did little to soothe their ever-festering wounds.

But perhaps it was fitting for a city steeped in Catholicism, whose team's very name evoked images of the men and women who made the ultimate sacrifice. Saints fans could perceive themselves as martyrs of a different sort, bearing the crucifix of gridiron defeat so that others might find Super Bowl salvation.

Worst of all, despite being the purported leader of this outfit, Radke had all but given up faith and was seeking refuge in the bottom of a bottle when the Divine intervened.

"Aw, heck, Ron, you know I was raised a Lutheran," Radke said to the team's owner, whose response he found a pleasant surprise. "Well, if the Pope himself doesn't care, bring him over. We could use a miracle around here."

The last detail caught Radke off guard and caused him to sit upright in his chair. "What?

He's already here? Yes, yes sir. I'm on my way."

Radke hung up the phone and instinctively reached into his shirt pocket for the breath spray that would cover his tracks, even though he had not walked down Whiskey Road on this particular morn'. Limping out to the practice field – his bum knee acting up again – Radke stopped still when he saw the congregation huddled around what almost looked like a clear glass football helmet on wheels.

The PopeMobile was an engineering marvel in itself. Having been created after the failed 1983 assassination attempt in Vatican Square, the vehicle featured an exterior shell of molded, bullet-proof plexiglass mounted on the chassis of a Rolls-Royce.

It included a throne for the Pontiff to sit and a dais with cushioned armrests should he opt to stand. And it was equipped with all sorts of James Bond-ian gadgetry such as the automated holy water sprinkler, the holographic image projector (nothing more impressive than seeing the Pope's 40-foot-tall likeness splashed across the side of a building), the 14-speaker Bose Surround Sound PA system, and, of course, tear-gas dispensers just in case the adoring throngs of worshippers ever became a little too overzealous in attempting to demonstrate their love.

With the sound of a hydraulic seal being released, the PopeMobile's door slowly swung open, allowing an attendant to enter the cabin and assist the feeble man down the retractible steps and onto the cushioned ProTurf, where he was quickly surrounded by hulking players more than three times his size.

Pushing through to the front of the crowd, a diminutive bowling ball of a man with thinning hair and an expensive suit stepped before the Pope, while TV cameras recorded the scene.

"Your Holiness, it's truly an honor that you have graced us with your presence," he said, dropping to one knee and trying to kiss the Pope's hand. Rather than offering the hand, Pope Pius XIII looked quizzically at his lieutenants before patting the little munchkin atop his balding pate and muttering something indecipherable.

"Your Holiness," said Archbishop Boudreaux, "this is Mister Ron Beauchamp, the owner of the New Orleans Saints football team."

The Pope frowned and gestured for Beauchamp to rise to his feet. Having been briefed on the team's ignominious history, including the most recent controversy stemming from Beauchamp's threat to move the team to Los Angeles, the Pope's visit had taken on missionary-sized proportions.

Speaking in a barely audible voice, His Holiness motioned for a pigskin. Gripping the ball in his shriveled hands, he held it close to his nose so that he could take in the rich smell of genuine leather. He closed his eyes and smiled, then removed one hand to make the sign of the cross over the ball and mutter yet another blessing in a foreign tongue.

"His Holiness was quite a football player in his younger years back in Italy," Boudreaux said.

The Pope nodded, then lifted the ball with both hands and bounced it lightly off his forehead, giving a playful smile that showed the child inside of him was still alive and well.

"Football is life, yes?" he said to Beauchamp, growing solemn in his tone.

The gravity of the Pope's words caught the savvy team owner off guard, and he chuckled nervously. "Well, of course it is, Your Holiness, especially the way our fans react. It sure as heck isn't a business, at least a profitable one."

Beauchamp alone found this humorous, for, amid the debate over the team, the *Daily Doubloon* had published an investigative exposé revealing that the Saints organization had not only reaped $30 million in profit over the last fiscal year, but more importantly, since Beauchamp purchased the franchise in the mid-80's for upwards of $65 million, the team's market value had grown tenfold.

The Pope looked deep into Beauchamp's eyes and placed a hand on his shoulder. "Football...is like....religion," he said, choosing his words with utmost care. "It helps bring mankind together. It is not a business."

Beauchamp snickered. "Well, as my friends in the nonprofit world say, 'If there's no margin, there's no mission.'"

He looked to the Archbishop to help defuse the situation. "Archbishop, did you put him up to this? You did, didn't you." Beauchamp turned back to the Pope. "That Archbishop, he's a real kidder, that one, and quite a big football fan, I might add." The Pope glared. "Look, you want a donation for the Archdiocese? I'm sure we can arrange something."

Ignoring Beauchamp's blather, the Pope leveled a piercing gaze at him and spoke in barely a whisper. "For what shall it profit a man if he shall gain the whole world and lose his own soul?"

The brash businessman in Beauchamp reared his ugly head, and he laughed again, this time in defiance. "You came all this way just to tell me not to move my football team? With all due respect, Your Holiness, let's make a deal: you don't tell me how to run my football team, and I won't tell you how to run the Church."

Despite being raised in a devout Catholic family and having graduated from St. Aloysius in 1945, Ron Beauchamp had fallen from the church and chosen not to get up. He'd raised himself out of poverty to become the wealthiest man in all of New Orleans on the success of his manufactured home business, Beau Maison

Homes, and related housing developments. He'd been blessed with a talent for making money. He'd contributed millions to countless charitable causes. But he'd be damned if he was going to let anyone, even Pope Pius XIII himself, strong-arm him in his business affairs.

The gasps of shock were understandable, but Beauchamp's behavior was not without precedent. In recent weeks, amid his tussle to negotiate a new stadium deal, he had managed to hack off the governor, the mayor, the entire state legislature, the city council, the editorial board of the *Daily Doubloon* and, worst of all, the people of New Orleans.

Sensing things tumbling downhill, Jake Radke stepped into the fray and slapped Beauchamp on the back like they were the best of friends, even though they were blood enemies. The last thing Radke needed, with his team on the verge of yet another disastrous season, was the most revered religious leader in the world cursing their collective fate and condemning them all to hell.

"You'll have to forgive ol' Beach here, Your Holiness," Radke said. "Sometimes he gets to drinkin' his own bathwater and thinkin' it's champagne. What's say we introduce you to the team?"

"Yes, let's," Boudreaux said, also wanting to move the proceedings along. "We have to get His Holiness over to the casino by noon."

Radke lined up the team and introduced them one by one. Many players matched the Pope's distinct gestures with their own public displays of piety, which had become commonplace after sacks, interceptions, touchdowns, and other big plays.

"This here is Ezekiel Robinson," Radke said. Despite dwarfing the Pope at 6-foot-2 and 315 pounds, the third-year defensive tackle out of Notre Dame was genuinely awestruck at being in the presence of the Pope. With trembling hands, Zeke held out his trusted knee brace.

"*In nominè Patris et Filii et Spiritus Sancto, Amen,*" the Pope said, bowing to kiss the brace.

"And this here is Rahim," Radke said. "He's one of those Muslims...but he's okay."

"Rahim Muhammed Al Rashid," the man formerly known as Jermaine Cooper said, bowing before the Pope. "*Asa lama lakum.*"

The procession arrived at a beefy young man still wearing his football helmet. The dreadlocks flowing from beneath the helmet and and his mirrored face shield created a menacing effect.

"And this here is...Cedric would you take that damn helmet off," Radke said.

From behind the plastic shield a soft, high-pitched voice replied, "I'd prefer to leave it on if you don't mind. I'm feeling a bit sensitive today."

Radke turned to his guests to explain. "Boy's been sulking since draft day. If you ask me, he's off his meds again." He waved everyone along.

"This is our quarterback, Robbie Gauthier," Radke said, coming upon the strapping, 6-foot-4 Cajun from nearby Terrebonne Parish. Before the Pope could issue his blessing, a portly woman popped out from behind Gauthier and practically gave him a bear hug.

"Aw *cher*, soon as my Robbie call to tell me he was meetin' da Pope, I hop inna' caw and make a bee line for dis place," the woman said.

"Pope, dis is my momma, Miss Sandy Gauthier," the quarterback explained. "She's a real big fan."

Before Robbie could get his words out, Sandy had thrust a rosary into the Pope's hands. "If ya could bless dat, it would mean da world to my NèNè," she said. "She's on her deathbed now back in Cocodrie. Oh, and if ya could say a prayer for my husband, Benny. Dat would be good, too. His gout's been flarin' up somethin' bad, yeah."

Though impressed by Sandy's devotion, Archbishop Boudreaux recognized the need to pick up the pace. He gave the Pope a gentle nudge just as he wrapped up his blessing, before Sandy could pull out her digital camera for a souvenir photo.

Backup quarterback Kirk Wharton stood next in line holding a Bible. Since kicking cocaine, alcohol, painkillers, and sex addiction five years ago, the 12-year veteran had found salvation by taking up with an obscure fundamentalist Pentacostal sect that worshipped out of an abandoned bowling alley on Airline Highway.

He handed the Bible to the Pope as though the holy man had never seen the book. "You know, sir, it's not too late," Wharton said.

"*Excusè?*" the Pope said.

"To be saved," Wharton said. "John, chapter three, verse seven...'Ye must be born again.'"

"Come again?" Archbishop Boudreaux said.

"To become reborn, in Christ," Wharton said. "There's still time. 'Believe on the Lord Jesus Christ, and thou shalt be saved.'"

"Jesus, Mary, and Joseph," Radke screamed. "Wharton, will you shut the hell up for once? You're talkin' to the goddamn Pope here, not some Bourbon Street crack whore."

Catching himself, Radke offered a quick apology. "Sorry about the foul language, Your Holiness. I kinda' lose my head sometimes. You can see what I gotta' put up with."

"It is okay, my son," the Pope said to Radke. He then turned to Wharton, laying a hand on the Bible. "We all walk a different path but reach the same destination."

"Well, let's find our path to the end of the line," Boudreaux said. "The casino awaits."

At long last, the entourage arrived at the final player, a skinny, disheveled young man who looked more like a street urchin than a professional athlete. His long brown hair and scruffy beard spilled out over an elaborate neck brace. He sported two black eyes and seemed barely cognizant of his surroundings. The sunlight peeking through the clouds created an eery backlighting, and just as the Pope met eyes with him, a single, radiant beam of light shone down on the man, illuminating his entire being in golden hues. The Pope's eyes grew wide, and he raised a trembling hand to his gaping mouth.

Fearing his esteemed guest was having some sort of cardiac episode, Archbishop Boudreaux rushed to his aid. His entire career flashed before his eyes. How humiliating to have the Pontiff drop dead while under his watch.

"What, Your Holiness? What is it?"

Radke also tried to assist. "This here is Oleg Adamowicz. He's our new kicker, from Poland. We like to call him 'The Leg.'"

The additional information did little to roust the Pope from his rapture. Radke turned to Boudreaux. "You said the Pope was a soccer fan, right? Maybe he recognizes Oleg from his professional soccer days. They say he was a pretty big star in Europe." Radke turned back to the Pope. "Would you like an autograph?"

Oleg stood unfazed by the incident, his eyes but tiny slits. His head hadn't stopped throbbing since being waylaid on the Dome turf several days earlier. But by all accounts, he had been fortunate. According to the team doctors, it was a small miracle that he was even standing, considering they'd lost a pulse at one point while treating him on the field, thus prompting use of the defibrilator. The two black eyes, a result of the vicious hit, were the least of his worries. Oleg's biggest concern at the moment was when the Vicodin he'd popped a few minutes earlier was going to kick in.

Using his escorts for support, the Pope slowly dropped to both knees, and tears began to run down his cheeks.

"*Iesu*," he whispered, his lip quivering.

"Is he not feeling well?" Radke said. "We can bring him a chair." He yelled to no one in particular. "Somebody get a chair or something."

Archbishop Boudreaux raised his hand for quiet, and he leaned closer to listen. The Pope had reached out with both hands and begun peppering Oleg's hand with kisses, while the kicker remained detached and impassive.

"*Iesu*," the Pope said.

"What?" Radke said.

Archbishop Boudreaux turned to the coach, equally bewildered by the display.

"*Iesu*," Boudreaux said. "It's Latin for Jesus."

Week 10
0 Wins, 8 Losses

So desperate were the Saints to get off the *shnide* that Ron Beauchamp left no option unexamined: firing the coaching staff, switching quarterbacks, changing the uniform colors, even changing the team's name.

Despite the Saints' history of futility, these last two proposals set off a furor of public opposition, especially when a local radio station conducted a survey that showed opinion running at 90 percent in favor of keeping the team in black & gold. As for the name, nothing else even came close. The people of New Orleans and the sad-sack Saints were stuck together like red beans & rice.

In the end, Beauchamp's accountant informed him that perhaps the most cost-effective (and inexpensive) change would be to the stadium's field. The old-style artificial turf was one of the last of its kind remaining in the league and had been reviled by every visiting player, every coach, and even the media. That Oleg's head had bounced off the turf like a Super Ball was but one indication of its many unforgiving qualities.

The turf was a magnet for injuries: torn ACLs, ruptured achilles, concussions, contusions, and the mother-of-all-rugburns. Worse still, it was considered a "fast track," which means it made any team with a speed advantage over the Saints (translation: all 29 other teams in the league) that much more difficult to stop.

Yup, the old turf had to go, and in its place, Beauchamp installed a state-of-the-art synthetic surface called QuikTurf, made from recycled tires. The field had longer blades of "grass" and a softer feel and, to the naked eye, looked remarkably similar to the real thing. Unfortunately, because Beauchamp had put in a rush order, the rubber hadn't been given ample time to set. After a special Friday walk-through at the Dome, it had already earned a dubious nickname: QuikSand.

Oleg was probably the only player on the team who wasn't complaining about the new turf, because its tacky texture gave him much needed traction for his plant foot. Besides, he had bigger problems on his mind, namely a lingering headache and a case of double-vision. But he certainly couldn't let on that he was less than 100 percent. As it was, the first-year, free-agent kicker was barely hanging on to his job. He'd only been signed three weeks earlier after starting kicker/punter Darrell Schexnaildre, a former first-round draft choice out of Texas A&M, had been sent to prison, convicted on seven counts of wire fraud after an online gambling scam he'd financed went south.

The last thing Oleg wanted was to be put on waivers. Having already washed out of the European soccer league, getting cut by the Saints would cost him his work visa and force a return to his native Poland to begin life over, a two-time has-been at the age of 32.

Following practice, Oleg was waiting at the bus stop outside the Dome along Poydras Avenue when veteran All-Pro wide receiver Dexter Douglass drove past in his tricked-out Cadillac Escalade.

Dexter had to do a double-take, the thought of a teammate riding the bus being so unfathomable. Then again, everybody in the NFL knew kickers were a different breed. Antisocial behavior, odd superstitions, and a comparative lack of muscle tone were the norm. The bizarre incident with the Pope, everyone figured, was par for the course. Still, feeling a bit sorry for the new guy and with rain clouds looming, Dexter pulled over to offer a ride.

"What's wrong with yo' car, 'Leg?" he said.

"Nothing wrong," Oleg said in his clipped, Eastern European accent. "I do not drive."

"Say what?"

"I do not own automobile. I use bus."

"The bus?" Dexter said in disbelief. "In this town? White boy like you get yo' ass jumped."

Oleg shrugged as though the thought had not even crossed his mind. "Bus is clean," he said. "Not break down like train in Poland."

Dexter laughed. "I'll show you clean. Hop in. I'll give you a ride."

Once inside the black, armor-plated vehicle with black trim, tinted windows and gold-plated, Davin rims, Oleg held his backpack in his lap, afraid to touch anything.

"Check this out," Dexter said, grabbing a remote control the size of a credit card. "Just got this installed last week." A trio of video screens flipped down from the ceiling in the back of the vehicle, and a fourth popped up in the center of the dashboard. An action movie played on the screen, although the sound was drowned out by the thumping bass playing on the Alpine sound system.

"Why do you need ?" Oleg said, pointing to the remote.

"Keep my hands free while I'm driving."

"Arms are too short to reach dashboard?"

Dexter laughed, interpreting the remark as a joke. Truth was, he'd received the video screens as part of a new endorsement deal he'd signed with a Korean-based electronics manufacturer looking to get a stake in the lucrative hip-hop market.

Seems Dexter was busted watching a movie on the sidelines on his own personal mini-DVD player in the fourth quarter of a recent blowout loss. The ensuing controversy, including countless replays of the scene on ESPN's SportsCenter and virtually every other media outlet in the country, spurred a bidding war among mini-DVD manufacturers for his services as company pitchman.

Oleg scanned the cockpit to investigate.

"Why watch TV when you drive?"

"Gotta' keep it real," Dexter said.

"Watching road while driving. That is real."

Dexter grinned again. "It ain't about me. It's about taking care of my guests. Being a good host. Which reminds me, where you need to go?"

"Not far. Corner of Tulane and Miro."

"Tulane and what? Man, don't you know you livin' in the heart of the ghetto?"

Oleg shrugged again. "So. I grew up in ghetto. Back in Warsaw. Feels like home. Besides, apartment is just down street from stadium and from practice field." He had a point, considering that the Dome was less than two miles in one direction, and the Saints' Metairie practice facility was a five-mile straight shot in the other, once Tulane Avenue turned into Airline Highway. "Is coming up on left. Look for sign."

The two rode in silence for a moment, except for the pounding rap music, before Oleg jumped.

"There. You missed it," he said. "You drive right past street."

"How I'm s'posed to know where to turn?"

Dexter said. "This ain't my 'hood."

"Read sign. Sign in middle of street."

Dexter rolled his eyes. "Thing so small, can't barely see it. Shoot."

"Guess you do not want lose place in movie," Oleg said in his now familiar deadpan manner, jutting his chin toward the dashboard-mounted DVD screen. This elicited a smile from Dexter.

"Relax, 'Leg. I'll flip a bitch right here."

Oleg gripped his armrests with all his might. "No flip. Just turn, please."

Dexter cackled, making the u-turn and then veering onto Miro. But his good humor turned to bewilderment upon arriving at Oleg's apartment, a neat shotgun duplex on a pothole-scarred street just off the avenue. While many players bought mansions in suburbs like English Turn and Ormond Plantation or downtown lofts in the Warehouse District, virtually no one chose to live in this manner. Even the short-timers on the practice squad found luxury apartments in suburbs like Metairie or Kenner. To Dexter, Oleg was as odd as they came, and he found it some-what amusing.

"My man, you mean to tell me this your crib?"

"Not crib. In New Orlyuns, is called shotgun."

Dexter shook his head, laughing.

"Thank you for ride," Oleg said, feeling the need to repay his teammate's generosity. "Would you like to come in for vodka? From Poland.

Much better than Russian swill."

Dexter's reluctance to accept the invitation stemmed more from fear that his car would be stolen than from any lack of fellowship. Watching Dexter's eyes scan the block, Oleg sensed his hesitation.

"Do not worry. Will be safe...in daytime."

"Aw hell," Dexter said, throwing the car into park. "I don't have to be at the restaurant for another hour anyway."

Dexter's side venture, a successful fried chicken restaurant called Double-D's, took its name from his on-field moniker: Dexter Douglass, hence "Double-D." What Dexter didn't know was that, behind his back, teammates and opponents referred to him as "Triple-D" for "Dyslexic Dexter Douglass." To anyone who spent any time with Dexter, it was readily apparent that, despite having "attended" Florida State for three years, he was functionally illiterate. The success of his restaurant was a testimony to his remarkable talent in the kitchen, to the business smarts of his faithful wife, Charlinda, and also to his dogged determination, a trait that carried over onto the field. In football speak, his motor never quit.

Before climbing out of the vehicle, Dexter reached into the glove compartment and produced a .44 magnum pistol, which he kept around for security when handling cash at the restaurant. Down the street, he could already see a trio of kids scampering toward the truck. They probably figured it was the local dealer, which meant there was money to be made.

Prior to ducking into the house, Dexter called out in his most menacing voice, usually reserved for opposing cornerbacks. "You kids touch my ride, I'm gon' have to use this," he said, brandishing the pistol to get their attention. "I'm gon' be watchin' from in there." He motioned to the house. Instantly, the children stepped back from the SUV as though an electronic field surrounded it. Dexter flashed Oleg a sly smile as he walked past him through the open door.

"You shoot children, you will go to jail," Oleg said. Dexter glared at him for a beat before Oleg caught on. "Oh, I get it. Is joke. Very funny. I get."

Although he grew up in biting poverty in rural Georgia, Dexter was taken aback upon entering Oleg's home. The expansive front room was empty, save for a mattress on the hardwood floor, a bare lightbulb hanging from the ceiling, and an oversized duffel bag with clothes spilling from it.

Oleg dropped his backpack on the floor beside the mattress and moved to the mantle above the filled-in fireplace on the side wall, where he lit several small candles for additional light.

"Have seat," Oleg said, before walking back into what must have been the kitchen. Dexter examined his two options: the floor or the mattress. He chose the floor. In the other room, he could hear the slamming of a refrigerator door and the clinking of ice cubes in a glass. Oleg returned quickly, holding a frosted bottle of vodka, two empty glasses, and a third glass of ice water. He set them all down on the floor and took a seat on the mattress.

"Brought glass of water if you need to wash down vodka. Water in New Orlyuns is excellent."

Dexter nodded. "Yeah, I got one of them water machines in my crib, too."

Oleg shook his head. "No, this from pipe." Excited, he held up the glass of ice water. "And look at this. Refrigerator make cubes. As many as you like. Is remarkable, yes?"

Dexter shook his head in confusion, watching Oleg pour two tall glasses of vodka. "'Leg, I don't get it. I thought you was a big soccer star over there in Europe. How come you live like this?"

Oleg's brow furrowed. "I only tell people I was star. Was really just, how you say, second-string. Besides, you have never seen apartments in Europe." He spread his arms wide. "This place is like castle."

"Ain't you got no TV, no stereo? What do you do to entertain yourself?"

Oleg picked up a book on the floor beside the mattress, a copy of *One Hundred Years of Solitude*, which he'd checked out at the city's Central Public

Library, also located on Tulane Avenue.

"A book?" Dexter said. "That's it?"

"Can only read one book at time."

Dexter took a long draw from his vodka, acknowledging the smoothness and motioning for a refill. Given his size and muscular density, his alcohol tolerance was through the roof.

"But you must have some money," Dexter said.

"Send money to family in Poland."

"Brothers and sisters?"

"Five brother, four sister, and father. Mother die many years ago." Oleg reached into his duffel and pulled out a ziploc bag stuffed with photographs. He sifted through them, handing photos, one by one, to his guest.

"This your house?" Dexter said, pointing to a stark row house on a desolate, gray street with smokestacks rising in the background.

"In Warsaw. Family still there. Except one sister in New York. I am saving to buy big house in country for my father."

Dexter nodded in approval, the liquor starting to seep into his bloodstream. An easy smile washed over his face. "'Leg, you alright."

"Yes, feeling much better now. Thank you."

"You know, first thing I did when I got my rookie signing bonus was buy my momma a house. Over in Valdosta where she stay. Eight bedrooms, one for each kid, pond out back 'cause she likes her catfish. Couple of acres. Best money I ever spent."

"You are good man, Triple-D," Oleg said, also starting to feel the effects of the vodka.

"Double-D," Dexter said. "Double-D."

"Yes, that is correct. Double-D. You are good man, Double-D. Take care of family." He poured them each another tall glass of vodka. "I want to do same. Hope to make father happy. He still does not approve of me."

"What you mean, not approve?"

Oleg turned his head and stared off in the distance at the flickering candles. "When I first go to play football, Mother was very sad. I was only 17 when I leave. Soon after, she become sick and die. Father blame me. He will not say, but I know. He never did approve of sport. Thinks all, how you say, 'cheap thrills.'"

"He want you to stay and work in a damn factory?" Dexter said. "I tell you what's cheap. Being poor. That's cheap."

Oleg shook his head. "Father is very religious. Thinks sport distract from spiritual life. He has strong beliefs. Does not care for material things... like me."

Dexter looked around the empty room in disbelief. "Ha! 'Leg, you a trip."

"He think I use football to run away from family, because I am ashamed of who I am."

"He can't see you just tryin' to better yourself?"

"Cannot change man's head," Oleg said,

"unless you change his heart."

"Drop a new house on your old man, he gon' change his heart, believe me."

Encouraged, Oleg sat upright. "You think?"

"You and me," Dexter said, "we ain't all that much different. You a nigga' just like the rest of us. Just from the other side of the world."

This piqued Oleg's curiosity. "What is nigga'? I hear this word much in locker room."

"Nigga' like, like, what you call a brother when he your friend. Like, 'Whassup, my nigga'?'"

Oleg nodded, comprehending. "Ahh, is good to be nigga', yes? I would be happy to be your nigga'. Maybe I am first ever nigga' from Warsaw."

"Probly so, 'Leg. Just be careful who you call that. Some brothers don't take kindly to a white man usin' that word."

Oleg frowned. "I do not understand."

Dexter savored his vodka before explaining. "Used to be, nigga' mean slave. Or 'bout anything else a white man want. But we took it back. Now it mean whatever *we* want. 'Cause it's ours."

"I see. Sound much like my people. Nazis try to kill us all in concentration camp. But we survive."

Dexter whistled and shook his head. "Like I said,'Leg, you a nigga' just like the rest of us. Hell, Jesus was a nigga'. First nigga' out there. You see what they done to him. But you know what? Come a time when a brother gotta' quit runnin' and just be who he is."

He pushed himself to his feet, picked his gun up off the floor and slipped it into the waistband of his slacks. "But right about now I gotta' be leavin'. Thanks for the pop. Time for me to get over to the restaurant. Come on over anytime you wanna' eat."

Oleg stood with him. "Thank you. I will. Do you serve goat?"

"Goat?"

"Is my favorite. Lamb is good, too."

"Brother, we got frog legs, chicken gizzards, cow tongue, pig's feet, and pork jowls, but we ain't got no goat."

"Maybe I show you how to make. You will like. I promise."

"Bring it on. I'll try anything once." Turning for the door, Dexter held out his fist, waiting for his new friend to reciprocate.

"Yes, I see you do this in end zone with other teammates. Will you teach?"

Dexter grabbed Oleg's right fist and tapped it against his own from the top, then the bottom, then straight on. Next, he made the sign of the cross, pressed the palms of his hands together as though in prayer and bowed toward his new friend like a karate student preparing to spar.

"Farewell, my nigga'," Oleg said. "Or as we say in Poland, '*Do widzenia.*'"

The ritual complete, Dexter walked out the door to find his beloved Escalade jacked up and missing two of its gold-plated rims.

***

Given the strange events during the bye week – what with the Pope's visit and his miraculous jackpot win on dollar slots at the casino (which he donated to the Archdiocese) – you could forgive the local media for going overboard with the clichés after the Saints' last-second, come-from-behind win over the divisional archrival Atlanta Falcons.

"HAIL MARY," screamed the giant headline in Monday's edition of the *Daily Doubloon*.

"Bless you, boys," sang a gospel choir in a television commercial that was rushed into production after the victory.

"St. Dexter," callers on local talk radio began hailing the aging wideout who made the game-winning, tip-drill catch amid a swarm of opposing players. Granted, it was just one win. But you give a starving man ground beef, it tastes like filét mígnon.

Even Oleg was able to get in on the act. His head stopped spinning just enough to connect on field goals of 26 and 39 yards in the course of the comeback. But it was not without incident. Asked for a post-game comment, Oleg, caught up in the moment, forgot Dexter's advice and sparked a minor controversy by dedicating his effort "to all my niggas' in New Orlyuns."

Week 11
1 Win, 8 Losses

By the time Ron Beauchamp's press conference rolled around to announce his proposal for a
new football stadium, the plan had become the
worst-kept secret in New Orleans.

With each retelling it became more and more
preposterous: they were going to implode the
Superdome on live television and use the footage
for a new movie filming in town; they wanted to
plop the new stadium smack in the middle of the
French Quarter; they wanted to build a stadium
on the world's largest barge, float it along the
Mississippi River, and include a casino next door.

When Beauchamp actually spoke, you could
tell from the looks on the faces of the reporters
crammed into the press room at the team's
training facility that they were just the slightest
bit disappointed, although no one would dispute
the controversial nature of the plan.

Since completion of the Dome in 1975, the
Saints had enjoyed one of the most unusual

stadium deals in all of professional sports. First off, the State of Louisiana, which owned the stadium, covered all its operating expenses and allowed the team to use it rent-free.

Next, the Saints received all ticket revenue, plus about $10 million a year via parking, concessions, and other game-day revenue such as T-shirts, hats, banners, foam-fingers, and souvenir merchandise. Sales of luxury boxes, club seating, and all advertising within the Dome pumped in a few million more. Factor in the team's $80 million cut from the NFL's revenue-sharing program. Top it off with a $10 million direct cash subsidy payment from the state, and you had the recipe for a winning operation (at least financially). But it wasn't enough.

Beauchamp, who was the majority partner in a group of investors that bought the team in 1986 for $65 million, now single-handedly controlled an asset worth at least $600 million. With Los Angeles currently seeking to lure the NFL back to town (and with the NFL hoping to bring pro football back to the country's No. 2 media market), Beauchamp knew he held all the cards in this negotiation. If the governor wouldn't meet his demands, he'd be *forced* to take the team to Tinseltown.

Governor Jeanette Fontenot, the first female governor in the state's history, was backed into a corner. On the one hand, she had to prove herself as a shrewd negotiator in representing the people's interest. On the other, even though the Saints' deal made little sense from a financial perspective, the emotional impact of an NFL franchise – even one with a past as checkered as the Saints – was virtually impossible to put a price tag on.

Looking every bit his 77 years, Beauchamp stepped to the microphone, dressed in a black suit with a butter-yellow shirt and gold-patterned tie. Wisps of wavy white hair defied the Brylcream slicking it back and taunted the onlookers.

"I wanna' thank y'all for comin' out here today," Beauchamp said in his gravelly Irish Channel accent. "Since we poichased the team 10 years ago, we've been committed to providin' you with the best quality football team that money can buy. But the Nooawluns Saints are more than just a football team. They're a part of the fabric of this community. I want you to believe me when I say that, in my hawt, I want to do everything I can to keep this team here, where it belongs. I don't want to move the team, and I don't want to sell.

"But in recent years, the business climate in the National Football League has changed. We've seen 22 new stadiums built over the last 10 years, and because of that, the economics of fielding a competitive organization have changed.

"Now I don't need to remind you that Nooawluns is one of the smallest NFL markets, and we don't have the base of Fortune 500 companies located here to support the team the way other clubs do. The Superdome is a fine facility, and it's served its purpose over the years. No other stadium has hosted as many Super Bowls – nine. But its day has passed. In order to remain economically competitive, we need a new, state-of-the-awt facility that will enable us to create additional streams of revenue. So something's gotta' give.

"Today marks an excitin' day in the history of this franchise, because today, we're going to present to you our vision of the future. To assist in the presentation, I'd like to introduce our Vice President of Finance, Mister Byron Fielding."

Fielding, a tall, slender man with big eyes and a bulging Adam's apple stood beside Beauchamp like the lackey that he was and fiddled with a laptop computer that had been positioned on the podium. He signaled to someone in the back of the room to dim the lights and launched into a PowerPoint presentation, complete with its own theme music, a Dixieland variation of "When the Saints Go Marching In."

Using splashy computer graphics and animation, Fielding outlined the team's declining financial fortunes and made a compelling case for the new stadium. The naming rights alone, he said, would generate $3 to $5 million from a corporate sponsor. The abundant club seating and bevy of luxury suites, he explained, would provide the additional cash necessary to sign free agents on the open market.

"The problem," Fielding said, "is that exploding free agency in the early 1990s and the influx of new stadiums in the last 10 years have turned the Saints from one of the best franchises because of their fan support to one of the worst in terms of gross revenue."

The solution: All Saints Field. At an estimated cost of $450 million, the 75,000-seat, retractible-roof stadium would combine the best modern design elements with the traditional aesthetics that make fans feel at home.

"We've identified a tract of land that the City of New Orleans has expressed interest in redeveloping and would be willing to consider a tax abatement and incentive program," Fielding said. "This particular piece of property is located at the intersection of North Rampart and Bienville Streets, adjacent to the French Quarter and the Central Business District."

"Say, wait a minute," a familiar voice came from the crowd. It belonged to Lonnie Benedetto, better known as "Lonnie B," longtime sportscaster, talk show host and all-around thorn in the side of the Saints organization. "Isn't that the Iberville Housing Project?"

Fielding looked up from his computer and laughed nervously.

"Why yes, uhh, I'm glad you brought that up," he said, unconsciously straightening his tie and brushing the lint from his jacket. "That leads right into the next segment of our presentation and perhaps the most exciting aspect.

"The construction of All Saints Stadium creates a unique opportunity to offer the residents of the Iberville Housing Development," he said, "an all-expenses-paid relocation into a brand-new, deluxe resort community. Simultaneous to the construction of the stadium, we will be creating Beau Maison Gardens, the world's largest manufactured home resort on a parcel of land in New Orleans East that's also been targeted by the city for redevelopment."

"Where's this one located?" another voice from the crowd shouted.

"Almonaster and Read Boulevard."

This time Lonnie B shot to his feet. "You mean the old city dump?"

Fielding lifted his hand to quell the uprising. "Please. I believe 'landfill' is the proper term, and I can assure you that every measure has been undertaken to remediate any residual toxicity on the site. It's a really beautiful piece of land. Go out and see for yourself. The palm trees are set to be planted as soon as we sign the agreement."

"Well, what about the cemetery?" said Skeet Finley, a reporter for the *Daily Doubloon*.

"What cemetery?" Fielding said.

"St. Louis No. 1 is one of the most historic cemeteries in the country, and it happens to be right next to the housing project you want to tear down. What are you going to do about that?"

Eyes lighting up, Fielding smiled and clicked to the next slide, confident in his response.

"Yes, good point, Skeet. As you can see from this illustration, we're going to turn the cemetery grounds into a sort-of theme park area, with booths and vendors, rides, games, and other attractions. Imagine a fairgrounds where fans can come several hours before the game for tailgating and family fun."

"You mean you're gonna' pave over the cemetery?" Finley said.

"Oh no," Fielding said. "We'll leave the tombs and burial markers in place."

"Rides and games?" said another reporter.

"Family fun?" said a third, staring blankly.

"I'm sure you know that St. Louis No. 1 is the fourth most popular tourist attraction in the city. We'll be enhancing an already valuable asset and, hopefully, revitalizing the entire surrounding neighborhood, which, I'm sure you know, has suffered more than its share of crime and blight in recent years."

You could see Fielding's chest swell in pride over the good deed he and Beauchamp were offering to undertake for the people of New Orleans. Not wanting to miss out on the credit,

Beauchamp leaned over to make a comment.

"It's that kind of out-of-the-box thinking that is going to make this project so special," he said, "and a model for other cities around the league."

"Out of your mind is more like it," someone in the crowd muttered, sending a wave of laughter washing across the room.

At this point, things really began to go south for Beauchamp, Fielding, and the rest of their carefully constructed plans.

"Okay, so let me see if I got this right," Skeet Finley called out.

"Please, if you'll just let me finish the presentation," Fielding said, "we'll open up the floor for questions as soon as we're through."

But the press corps was having none of it.

"You want the taxpayers of Louisiana to build a new stadium, pay for its management, and give you all of the cash flow," Finley said.

"And you want the people of New Orleans to tear down a housing project and move its residents to the world's largest trailer park, which is built on the old city dump?"

"Precisely," Fielding said, crossing his arms in smug satisfaction.

"*And* you want to turn a historic cemetery into an amusement park?" Benedetto said.

"We like to refer to it as a multi-dimensional entertainment complex," Fielding said.

"How much of your own money is the Saints

organization going to put up for this project?" an attractive female television reporter asked.

Beauchamp didn't want to touch that. Better to throw Fielding under the bus.

"Based on the model we've created," Fielding said, "we intend to finance the deal with public funds, given the long-term economic benefits to the city and state."

"So, according to your plan, the Saints aren't going to be paying for any of it," Benedetto said.

"We prefer to think of it as an investment in the continued economic vitality of the region."

"All at the taxpayer's expense," Finley said.

Fielding's eyes darted to Beauchamp. "Well, uhh, technically, that would be correct."

With this reply, gasps and whispers turned into all-out laughing. Sensing control slipping away, Beauchamp stepped to the rescue.

"This seems to us an equitable investment in a corporation that yields $181 million in economic impact annually and a projected $12 billion over 25 years," Beauchamp said. "Plus, you can't even begin to quantify the impact from hosting the Super Bowl, not to mention the psychological benefits to Saints fans."

"Can you elaborate on the psychological benefits of rooting for a lousy team?" some young punk reporter from the local ESPN radio affiliate shouted. Beauchamp chose to ignore that particular question but was broadsided by another one just as vexing.

"Can you say if there are any other teams that have been able to get a new stadium without putting up a portion of their own money?" a scribe from the *Baton Rouge Daily News* asked.

"There are many examples of public-private partnerships around the league, but every case is unique," Fielding said. "I can't speak to the specifics of any other teams."

"You say you need this new stadium in order to generate enough revenue to remain competitive," said a pesky investigative reporter from the flaming liberal weekly paper. "But isn't it true that the Saints had the highest payroll in the NFL last season and still finished 7-9?"

"That's a personnel question," Fielding said. "I'm an operations guy. I can't comment on that other than to say that we had a terrible time with injuries last season."

"But what about the larger issue?" the reporter continued. "If the Saints are in the NFL's smallest and poorest market, why should the taxpayers subsidize your operation so that you can operate at mid-level profitability compared to the rest of the league?"

This was about all Fielding could take from someone who was obviously a communist. The insolence. The hostility. How dare these people question their noble intentions.

"Look, we've had 38 years of lousy football

in this city," Fielding said. "We want to do
everything we can to make sure we have 38
more."

Somehow that didn't quite come out right. He
looked to Beauchamp for backup, but before a
retraction could be issued, another question was
knocking at the door.

"In order to continue doing business with the
state, are you willing to open your financial
records to the legislative auditor's office, as
Governor Fontenot has insisted?" the female TV
reporter said.

Beauchamp had seen enough. A scowl on his
face, he pushed Fielding out of the way and
gripped the microphone so his words could be
heard by all.

"The Nooawluns Saints been doin' business
with the State of Louisiana for more than 30
years without openin' our books to them," he
said. "We're not going to stawt now.

"Governor Fontenot has a clear choice to
make. She can accept what we think is a very fair
offer, or she can tell us to leave. Simple as that."

With that pronouncement, Beauchamp tugged
at Fielding's sleeve, indicating they were done.

"Thank you for coming today, ladies and
gentlemen," Beauchamp said. "This concludes
today's conference."

Before any final questions could be posed, the
duo disappeared behind a locked door, leaving

the assembled truth-seekers to find the answers for themselves.

A lone Saints PR flak stood at the ready, trying to put the best spin on the situation, but no one wanted to talk to him. Thus began a desperate search for someone, anyone who would provide context, perspective, or heck, just a spicy quote to top off this already hot story like a shot of Tabasco on a plate of jambalaya.

Catching a glimpse of Oleg exiting the weight room just off the main hall, Skeet Finley called out to get his attention. After his inadvertant racial slur, Oleg had become a fast favorite among local reporters for his colorful, if understated, take on the Saints. In seconds, the media circus had descended upon the unsuspecting kicker as though he were an expert on the intricate workings of NFL finance.

"Hey 'Leg, what do you think of Beauchamp's new proposal?" Finley said.

"Do not know much about it," Oleg said.

"Come on, 'Leg," Finley said. "You must have an opinion on it. This is America. It's a free country. You can speak your mind. Do you agree that the state should put up all the money for the new stadium?"

Oleg shrugged. "Is no big deal. In Europe, state own many sport team. Is good for people."

"But if the state puts up the money, do you think it's fair that Beauchamp will get all the profit?" Lonnie B jumped in.

Oleg squinted to try and understand. "Wait a second. Is rich already, Mr. Beauchamp, yes?"

"Well, of course he is," Lonnie B said. "He's paying your salary, isn't he?"

Oleg pointed his finger in the air in order to track his thoughts. "If rich already, then why does he need more money?"

"What you tryin' to say?" Lonnie B said.

"Why not own team just for sport? For good of New Orlyuns."

"Aw 'Leg, that ain't how it works," Lonnie B said. "This is America. You know, capitalism an' all dat. You not in Poland no more."

Oleg nodded and smiled, indicating that he understood. "Ah yes, I see. Is like peeg."

The gathered wordsmiths checked with each other to interpret that last offering.

"Peeg?"

"Well, maybe is more like hog," Oleg said.

"Hog," Lonnie B said. "I get it. Hog."

"Yes, hog," Oleg said. "Is more like hog. You know, get fat, wallow in filth. Like hog."

"Well, what'cha think of that," Skeet Finley said, "Beauchamp bein' a hog and all?"

Oleg pondered the question. The reporters stood with tape recorders and pencils poised. "In my country we have saying, 'Pig get fat...but hog get slaughtered.'"

Not knowing whether Oleg was joking or

serious, the crowd burst in guffaws despite knowing full well the poor sod had just sealed his doom with the team.

***

When Oleg saw the newspaper the following morning, his heart leapt with excitement.

Certainly, he'd seen his name in the paper and been quoted countless times, but never like this. All those things he'd heard about America being a free country were true, and here was proof, in the headline at the top of Page A1:

'IS LIKE PIG'
Saints Propose Feeding at Public Trough,
Beauchamp unveils plan for new stadium

Oleg was so tickled, he didn't even notice the way everyone kept their distance down at the training facility, Coach Radke having already issued a gag order to keep anyone else from running afoul of the team owner. Quarterback Robbie Gauthier was just about the only person who would speak to him, and that was only because he still served as Oleg's holder, despite being promoted to starting QB five weeks earlier.

The lone reason Beauchamp didn't order Radke to cut Oleg on the spot was that there wasn't enough time to bring in a replacement before the next game. Knowing Oleg's days were numbered, Gauthier wanted to give him some kind of warning. But Oleg had been so darned upbeat lately, and it was carrying over into his kicking. The last thing Gauthier wanted to do was mess with Oleg's head before a game.

Oblivious to the looming threat, Oleg couldn't wait to get on the field against the New York Jets that Sunday. Since the effects of the concussion had worn off, he'd felt like a new person. His strength had not only returned, it seemed to have doubled. His eyesight improved, as did his mental focus. And he had become as limber as a ballet dancer. Although he refrained from doing so in the presence of other men, he could now execute full frontal and side splits as well as pull his foot up and wrap it behind his head. The combination of strength and flexibility made his kicking leg feel like a Howitzer, translating on the field to easy conversions from 55 and even 60 yards, giving Gauthier further reason to keep his mouth shut.

Good move.

***

The following day, in front of a lethargic Superdome crowd of 49,000, despite three Gauthier interceptions, the Saints found themselves down only 23-21 with the ball and good field position at the 2-minute warning.

Gauthier hit Jordash Jones for a 17-yard gain with 1:39 left on the clock, putting the Saints at the Jet 35-yard-line. But on the next play, offensive guard Clarence Porter was flagged for holding, and then a botched exchange from center forced them to burn their final timeout.

On third-and-23, Gauthier took a deep drop and was preparing to hit a wide-open receiver flashing over the middle, when an opposing linebacker caught him from his blind side on a delayed blitz.

With fourth-and-42 and time ticking away, Radke called for his kicker. A gambling man, Radke knew the odds of pulling off a Hail Mary two weeks in a row were a million-to-one. An NFL-record-breaking 69-yard field goal, on the other hand, just might work.

As Radke ordered the kicking team onto the field, Beauchamp sidled up to him, arms crossed, frowning.

"Soon as he misses this kick, cut him," Beauchamp said. "I don't even want him back in the locker room. Get him outta' here."

Fortunately, amid the chaos of the moment and the suddenly deafening crowd noise, Radke did not hear his boss' mandate.

Instead, as he and Beauchamp stood side by side watching the ball sail through the uprights, they saw a new star being born.

Week 12
2 Wins, 8 Losses

Being the man of the moment, Oleg couldn't refuse Jordash's invitation to the team's regular postgame convocation at The Skyline Lounge, the city's glitziest bar & nightclub, located on the top floor of the chic X Hotel in the Warehouse District. But after a couple of celebratory toasts, Oleg found himself back on the sidelines, watching the action on the playing field, or in this case, the dance floor.

Spotting an empty seat in the corner of the room, Oleg joined Cedric Wilson, the burly, dreadlocked running back, who sat on an opposing Eames chair, eyes closed and legs crossed in the lotus position. Oleg remained there, silent for several moments before Cedric acknowledged his presence.

"Why do you not dance like others?" Oleg said.

Cedric shrugged and replied in an impossibly mousy voice for someone of such prodigious muscularity. "Not my scene," he said, glancing at the bodies gyrating on the dance floor. "To tell you the truth, I don't even know why I'm here."

"Then why come? Why not go home?"

"Not *here*," Cedric said. "*Here* here." He waved his hands through the air to take in the entirety of the surroundings.

Oleg searched the room to interpret his meaning before figuring it out.

"Ah, you mean New Orlyuns. I see." Oleg cocked his head, seeming to re-evaluate the statement, and he shrugged. "I do not know. New Orlyuns is not so bad."

"Come on, 'Leg. Haven't you noticed since you got here? It's rainy. It's dirty. It stinks. And it ain't safe. I can't stand it."

This confused Oleg. "But you are sitting."

Cedric ignored the rebuttal and pressed on. "Man, nothing feels right in this place."

Oleg took a sip of his vodka and looked out of the plate-glass window at the illuminated cityscape. "Many places you must go, you will not like," he said, still facing outward. He then returned his eyes to Cedric. "Wise man say, 'The Perfect Way is only difficult for those who pick and choose. Do not like. Do not dislike. All will then be clear.'"

A look of desperation covered Cedric's face. "But it's so hard, especially with my sad."

"Everybody get sad sometime," Oleg said.

"No, my 'sad.' S.A.D. Seasonal affective

disorder. It's been raining so much since I got here. Seems like every day. And it makes me depressed. The doctors gave me some medicine for it, but it doesn't work. The only thing that does the trick is *ganja*, but that slows me down too much."

Oleg stared at Cedric for an awkward beat before finally smiling. "Oh, I get. You, too, are good at joke. Very funny."

Cedric unfurled his legs and planted them on the floor so he could stand to face Oleg. "It's not a joke. The doctors diagnosed it last week. Ever since I left L.A., I haven't felt right. It's just been so gloomy here all the time."

Oleg stood to meet him face to face. "So you are serious?" Cedric nodded. "Then I have word of advice, my friend. Stay away from Warsaw. You will want to put gun to head on second day."

Cedric slapped him on the shoulder, and his eyes lit up for the first time since the conversation began. "See, you do understand."

Oleg nodded. "Okay, I understand. I guess I have sad too one time."

"Really? What'd you take for it?"

"You Americans, you want to take pill for everything. There is no pill for sad."

"But what did you do?

"Same thing you must do. You cannot make sun shine out here." He waved his arms in a circle. "Until you move cloud out of brain." He pointed to his head.

"'Leg, man, you are blowing my mind," Cedric said. A look of awe covered his face. "Can you show me how?"

"Not sure how to blow mind."

"No. The cloud. Tell me how to move it."

Oleg smiled and nodded. "Ah, my friend, I can tell, but only you can do for yourself."

Cedric's head bobbed up and down like an eager puppy. "Okay, I will. I promise."

As Oleg prepared to bestow his sage wisdom upon Cedric, a shrill voice cut through the air to interrupt them.

"Excuse me, Alex."

Oleg turned to find two beautiful women, a statuesque brunette and her leggy black friend.

"Pardon?" Oleg said.

"I'm sorry to botha' ya, Alex," the brunette said, "but I was wonderin' if ya could gimme' an autograph for my momma."

She thrust a piece of folded-up newspaper toward him, the previous day's issue of the *Daily Doubloon* that carried a photo of Oleg along with the caption in which he had compared Ron Beauchamp to swine.

"His name is Oleg," Cedric said, showing his irritation at having his road to enlightenment blocked. "Oleg, not Alex."

"Why you named after somebody's leg?" the black woman chimed in.

"He's from Poland," Cedric said, simmering.

"Ohhhh," the brunette said in a sing-song voice. "Gosh, I'm so embarrassed. Pawdon me. Where's my manners? My name's Charmaine, Charmaine Fontana. Dis here's my friend, Lexi."

Shawwwwmaine.

She held out her hand to shake Oleg's, and he was instantly enchanted by her exotic accent, not realizing that this bastardized, Pidgen variation of the English language was common among many New Orleanians, or "Yats" as they are known. In Oleg's eyes, she would have been absolutely perfect if not for her slightly crooked teeth, her excessive perfume and her heavy-handed touch with the makeup brush. Nonetheless, compared to most women of the Eastern Bloc, she was a knockout.

Cedric recognized the pair as members of the Saints dance team, The Saintsations, a group he regarded as only slightly more reputable than a den of French Quarter strippers.

"Next week is my momma's birthday, so I wanted to get her somethin' special," Charmaine said, "and den I opened da paper and saw ya picture, and, I swear, it looked jus' like da tatoo on her awm."

Oleg strained to listen closely. *Awm?*

"So I thought, 'Hey, why don'tcha get Alex to autograph his picture and put it in a little frame."

Oleg's eyes narrowed as his brain worked

overtime to process the information. "I'm sorry. You say I look like tatoo?"

"Of Jesus. On my momma's right shoulder," Charmaine said, pointing to the top of her own arm to show the exact location.

"You're her favorite at'lete now since she seen ya on da news last week," Charmaine said.

"When ya dropped the N-word," Lexi said. "We know you ain't meant it like that."

Charmaine powered on. "Momma says ya look jus' like Jesus wit' ya hair all long and dat beard and ya cheeks sunken in like ya been stawvin' ya'self a few weeks.

"She's been all depressed since she missed out on meetin' da Pope," she continued. "But I know dis'll cheer her up. And just in time for her birthday. How 'bout dat?"

Without waiting for a response, she jammed the newspaper into Oleg's hands along with a black Sharpie. While Oleg obliged her, Lexi struck up a conversation of her own with Cedric.

"I just love your hair," she said, stroking his long, matted dreadlocks. "Real dreadlocks on a brother are sexy."

"Really?" Cedric said like a shy schoolgirl. "You think so?"

"Yes indeed," Lexi said. "Especially on a fine lookin' black man like yourself."

"Aw, jeez, stop," Cedric said. "You're gonna' make me blush."

"Why y'all sittin' here in da corner," Charmaine said. "Let's all go out and dance."

Oleg looked to Cedric for permission. "Is up to him. I was just going to move brain cloud before you arrive."

Cedric hardly noticed, as the low pressure system in his head had already begun showing signs of weakening. Lexi had found the most direct route to his heart – through his hair. Suddenly, Cedric viewed the woman standing before him as pillar of virtue, as he did, by association, all the girls on the Saintsations squad, who were obviously on leave from the convent.

"Say, why don't we go dance like Charmaine said," Lexi said.

Cedric smiled and began to sing in an angelic voice. "I've got sunshine...on a cloudy day."

"Guess brain cloud clear up," Oleg said, shrugging. "Looks like we will dance."

***

Storms were still roiling inside Ron Beauchamp's head the following day when he burst into the team's film room to interrupt Jake Radke.

Around the league, it was well known that "The Anvil" spent an insane amount of time studying game film. He went so far as to sleep on a cot in his office an average of three nights a week, a fact that made his threadbare gameplans all the more perplexing.

A disciple of George "Papa Bear" Halas in Chicago during that team's glory years, Radke clung to offensive and defensive strategies that were embarrassingly simple, based on a run-oriented offense and a 4-3 defense. Sportswriters joked that a high school coach could outscheme him. And during games, opposing linebackers would go so far as to make bets on which play the Saints would run next. Judging by the team's abysmal 1.3 yard-per-carry rushing average and 54.6 quarterback rating, more often than not they guessed right.

But true to his nickname, The Anvil wouldn't bend. Whatever the Calumet City, Illinois, native lacked in brainpower, he made up for in his work ethic and a single-minded determination that some would read as stubbornness. Which is why he didn't take kindly to anyone questioning his decisions, even the team's owner.

Beauchamp positioned himself directly between Radke and the wide-screen television so he could have his coach's full attention.

"Morning, Jake," Beauchamp said. "Glad to see you're working hard, as usual."

Radke flicked off the digital video system and pushed toward Beauchamp a chair that looked a lot like an oversized school desk.

"What brings you here this bright and early?" Radke said. With the chaos that followed Oleg's game-winning kick, Beauchamp hadn't been able to get his point across about cutting the kicker.

"Some game yesterday," Radke said.

"Yes, it certainly was."

"I think we're starting to get on the right track. I want to thank you for your help."

"For my help? Why?" Beauchamp said.

"We're 2-0 since you brought the Pope out to meet the team."

"Oh don't be ridiculous. The Pope doesn't have anything to do with it. Just a little luck, is all. Something that's been in short supply around here for a long, long time."

Radke chuckled and shook his head. "You can believe whatever you want, but you know how superstitious football players are. Far as any of them are concerned, it was the Pope's visit. They think we got the man upstairs on our side."

"Please spare me the Billy Graham gospel hour," Beauchamp said. "I didn't come over here to be converted."

"Well then what the heck do you want? You know we got our work cut out for us on Sunday."

"I came over to talk about that stinkin' Polock kicker you got. I want him out of here."

"Excuse me? Are we talking about the same kicker who just broke Tom Dempsey's record?"

"Listen. Our negotiations with Governor Fontenot are at a very sensitive stage. The last thing we need is some loudmouth popping off over something he doesn't know anything about."

"You're just mad 'cause he called you a pig."

"This isn't about me. It's about the long-term financial viability of this team. You do want to keep your job, don't you?"

"You know the answer to that question."

"Then cut him...now."

Though hobbled by age and injury, Radke still possessed the stature and girth of a former offensive lineman. He walked to Beauchamp's desk and leaned forward, resting his weight on his bowling ball fists.

"With all due respect, sir, are you out of your mind? You got enough of a battle tryin' to tear down the projects and turn a city dump into a trailer park. You cut Oleg now and they'll be comin' with a rope for you and me both. That boy's become popular as Jean Lafitte."

Not that Beauchamp feared for his safety, but Radke's proximity and his reputation for violence did pose a palpable threat, altering his thought processes. Beauchamp breathed deep.

"Well, maybe you have a point."

Radke rose upright and smiled, sensing he'd preserved the lone glimmer of hope that his team had enjoyed in an otherwise dismal season. Beauchamp rose along with him, his mind infused with an acceptable compromise.

"I tell you what. I'll let you keep your kicker for now. But if I hear one more peep out of that kid, I won't just get rid of him. I'll be coming for you, too. Got it?"

The gulping sound in Radke's throat was audible. "Yes, sir."

Beauchamp laughed. "In the meantime, I think I'll conveniently forget to sign his paychecks. Season'll probably be over by the time that stupid bastard figures it out. What do they use for money in Poland anyway? Rubles?"

"You can't just not sign his paycheck."

Beauchamp smiled defiantly. "I can do whatever the hell I want. Remember, Jake, I own the team. Like the golden rule says, 'He who has the gold makes the rules.'"

"That ain't the golden rule."

"Hey, it works for me." Beauchamp patted Jake on the shoulder and prepared to leave. "Remember, keep that kid on a tight leash or else you'll both be in the doghouse."

***

Prompted by an El Niño weather pattern in the Pacific, summer had been ridiculously late in relinquishing its grip on the city of New Orleans. But in the days leading up to the game against Tampa Bay, the oppressive humidity and rainfall cleared out, replaced by cooler, drier air. As the change of seasons took full effect and autumn color took hold, many even speculated that this was the most beautiful fall in recent memory.

The effect was not lost on Cedric, who seemed like a new person, coming out of his shell to laugh and joke with teammates. He even consented to an interview without his helmet on.

The pattern continued in Tampa, where conditions were sunny and 78 degrees at kickoff, and Cedric regained the form that had carried him to a Heisman Trophy at the University of Southern California the previous year.

For once, Radke's old-school gameplan seemed to work, as Cedric was able to rack up 247 yards on 38 carries for a 6.5-yard average against what had been the league's premiere defensive unit.

Unfortunately, despite driving up and down the field all day long, the Saints couldn't score TDs in the red zone, mainly due to Gauthier's inefficiency at quarterback. Every time the Saints crossed their opponent's 30-yard-line, the Bucs loaded eight men in the box to stop the run and forced Gautier to beat him with his arm.

With the team continually unable to convert on third-and-long, Oleg was called on to work his magic. And he did not disappoint.

For the second consecutive week, Oleg brought down another NFL record with his leg, this time for most field goals in a game. Connecting on tries of 32, 27, 48, 39, 41, 55, 28, and 36 yards, the Saints cashed in a 24-20 victory.

Much to the dismay of the assembled media in the press room after the game, however, Oleg was unavailable for comment.

Week 13
3 Wins, 8 Losses

Ron Beauchamp sat in his office on the 47th
floor of One Shell Square in downtown New
Orleans, feeling queasy as he watched The
Weather Channel.

Yet another tropical system had developed in
the Atlantic Basin, plotting a course of destruction for the Caribbean before making its way into
the Gulf of Mexico, looking for a target like a kid
playing Whack-A-Mole at Chuck E. Cheese.

This particular storm was the 18th of the
season – a new record – and the latest to develop
in the Western Hemisphere since 1927. It had
quickly grown to hurricane strength, fed by the
still-warm ocean waters, and now its projected
path spanned from Key West to Galveston.

Practically any point of landfall, as far as
Beauchamp was concerned, would spell doom for
his Beau Maison enterprise. Hurricane season
had devastated the company, which not only
developed manufactured-home "resorts" all along

the Gulf Coast, from Texas to the tip of Florida. But more importantly, Beau Maison Insurance (known as BMI), at one time the true cash cow of the operation, had suffered heavy losses from the unprecedented string of natural disasters. Not merely from this hurricane season, but for two years running. One more big storm, and the resulting flood of claims could send his entire empire crashing down.

Compounding the agony, NOAA meteorologists had tagged the system with an ominous name: Hurricane Ronald. Just the added bit of irony needed to make an already cynical man hopelessly bitter, convinced that larger forces in the universe were conspiring against him.

Beauchamp reached into his desk and popped his blood pressure medicine, having suffered a heart attack five years earlier while dancing the "Beauchamp Boogaloo" on-field following a rare Saints victory. After a light knock on the door, Byron Fielding entered, carrying a spreadsheet, which he handed to Beauchamp.

"Well, how's it look?" Beauchamp said, drawing a deep breath as though bracing himself for a blast of bad news.

Fielding tried to look his boss in the eye. But after weighing the grim verdict, he dropped his head and stared at the carpet.

"Not good," he said. "I just don't know how we're going to do it."

"Come on, you're a Tulane boy. There's gotta' be a way."

"Ron, we've already funneled $30 million to BMI," Fielding said. "If we try to do any more, it's going to be obvious, at least as long as we've got the state auditors on our back."

"Well then get 'em off," Beauchamp said.

"Can't do that, not if you want the stadium deal to go through. And we need it, if we're going to restructure our long-term debt and save the whole Beau Maison operation, especially BMI."

"But BMI needs cash flow to hold off the creditors," Beauchamp said. "Claims are coming in faster now than they were a month ago. And now we got this." He pointed to the TV, where a graphic outlined the projected storm path.

"Hurricane Ronald," Fielding said. "That's too funny."

"Oh yeah, it's hilarious," Beauchamp said. "You can see how ecstatic I am."

"I'm sorry. It's just..."

"I'll tell you one thing. Tithing to the church...horrible investment." He looked up at the ceiling. "It's like that son of a bitch is out to get me." He looked back to Fielding. "What'd I ever do to deserve this, you tell me."

"You do realize you can't buy your way into heaven, don't you?" Fielding said.

"Ah what the hell do you know," Beauchamp said. "You're a Jew."

"That was uncalled for." Fielding shot up from his chair, a wounded look on his face, and walked to the window. "You Christians, you think you've got a monopoly on religion. Don't forget, your boy JC was a Jew."

"Let's get one thing straight," Beauchamp said, acting gravely offended. "I'm a Catholic... not a Christian."

Fielding paused for a moment as if to gather a modicum of courage. "You know, there is *one* way out of all this," Fielding said, staring out over the Central Business District and the Mississippi River in the distance. "You could just sell the team. You'll get six or seven hundred million from the Los Angeles consortium. Wipe away all your worries just like that."

Beauchamp grimaced as though he'd suggested selling his soul to Satan. "Never."

"You mean you'd rather go bankrupt?"

Beauchamp joined Fielding at the window, looking out, his hands in his pockets. "When I said I didn't want to sell this team, it wasn't just a negotiating ploy. I don't want to sell."

He turned to face Fielding. "I know you didn't grow up here, so I don't expect you to understand. But this team, it means more than just football. They got a lot of people in this city who have it rough. They work hard all week and then on Sunday, at least for three hours, they can forget all their problems and get a little enjoyment outta' the Saints. And for 30 years, all we been givin' 'em is a losing operation. Just once, I want to give 'em a reason to be proud, a reason to celebrate. Win the Super Bowl. Heck, make the playoffs. *That* would be something. To turn around and sell out before that day comes, to me, would be worse than going bankrupt."

"If you go broke, you won't have a team."

"I know it's not rational, but it's what I want. Before I owned the Saints, I was just a glorified used car salesaman. You think I don't know what they said about me behind my back? Please."

"Well, you did make those obnoxious TV commercials with that donkey," Fielding said.

This did nothing to thwart Beauchamp's momentum. "But when I bought this team, I certainly got their attention. Now...now, I'm somebody. This thing falls apart, they'll have a field day riding me out of town."

"Ron, who's 'they'?"

Beauchamp seemed to be staring down a bogeyman a thousand yards off. "I got rich by going with my gut," he said. "If I'm gonna' go broke, I'll do it the same way."

"Then what do you recommend we do?"

Beauchamp shrugged. "Pray?"

"But I thought you swore off religion."

"Prayer's about the only hope we got left, not that I really think anybody'll listen."

As the two stood in silence, the meteorologist

on the TV screen announced that, based on the latest computer model, Hurricane Ronald could soon be heading toward New Orleans.

***

"Dammit, Dexter," Charmaine said as she stared at the directions the wideout had given her to Oleg's apartment. Sitting in her Mazda Miata at the intersection of Canal and Carrollton, she found herself in unfamiliar territory. Not only was the Ninth Ward native unaccustomed to navigating the inner city, but she was also playing an unusual role, that of suitor.

Oleg had almost seemed immune to her womanly charms, and that intrigued her all the more. Certainly, he couldn't be gay. They didn't have homosexuals in Poland, she reasoned.

"It's against the law there," her mother had said. After receiving such a thoughtful birthday gift, Miss Shirley Fontana wanted nothing more than for her 27-year-old daughter to get to know the young man, even if he wasn't from the area. She wanted to do all she could to improve Charmaine's chances. So she armed her daughter with a unique proposition.

Charmaine had skipped out of her last class of the morning in the dental hygenist program at St. Bernard Parish Community College, hoping she'd catch Oleg before he left for practice. She hadn't counted on getting lost. But after a series of random turns, she came upon 227-B South

Miro, just as was written on her directions.

The detour did serve one useful purpose, however. The panic Charmaine felt at being lost in the 'hood distracted her from the butterflies in her stomach. So much so that when she knocked on Oleg's door, she almost felt calm.

But then, no answer.

"Dammit. I knew I should've come earlier," Charmaine cursed under her breath.

Wait a second. Were those footsteps? She leaned toward the door, cocking her ear to listen. Yes, those were footsteps. She knocked again.

Those definitely were footsteps, but it sounded like more than one pair. Maybe he has a roommate...wait, what was that? Was that a woman's voice? It definitely wasn't a man's.

Charmaine threw her head back and cast her eyes upward. "Oh great, Charmaine, you gone and done it now."

She almost wanted to turn and run back to the car and forget this ever happened. She took a step backward and was preparing to turn her shoulders when Oleg opened the door.

He stood wearing only a pair of soccer shorts. It was all Charmaine could do to keep from staring at his washboard abs and a pair of pecs that rose from his chest like a couple of cantaloupe halves. Whatever Oleg may have lacked in size, he more than made up for in proportion, and he had not an ounce of excess fat on his body.

"Hello," he said, his matted, wet hair falling down upon his shoulders. "I am sorry it take so long. Was in shower."

"Oh, it's my fault," Charmaine said. "I shoulda' called first, but I realized I didn't have ya number. So Dexter gave me ya address."

Oleg smiled and nodded. "Ah yes, Dexter is good nig...is good friend, very good friend."

Charmaine shifted her weight from one foot to ther other and brushed a lock of hair from her eyes. "I don't wanna' keep ya. I know ya got practice soon. But I wanted to aks ya somethin'."

"Yes, anything," Oleg said, his own heart racing. This was a most pleasant surprise.

"Well, after I gave my momma ya picture and all for her birthday, she mentioned somethin' dat got me thinkin'. Our church, St. Peter, down in Arabi, it ain't doin' so well."

"Arabi? You do not look like Arab."

Charmaine laughed. "No, Arabi. It's like a suburb of New Orleans, down in da Ninth Ward, downriver by Chalmette."

Oleg nodded.

"Anyway, Father Joe, who's da Pastor, he's a sweet man and all, and I know my momma'd do anything to help him. Well, we got to thinkin', wit' you bein' so famous, we thought you could come over to da church and sign autographs after mass next Sunday."

Oleg's brow furrowed as he weighed the offer. "But Sunday is game. I do not think..."

"Not dis Sunday. Next Sunday. It's da late game, 'cause y'all playin' on ESPN, remember?"

Oleg nodded, his memory aided.

"If you come for morning mass, you'll be outta' there by early afternoon. No problem."

"But how will autograph help?"

Charmaine smiled. "We can advertise all over da city and da people can make donations. Wit' da money we raise, we'll be able to keep da church open at least another month, at least till da Pope's slot machine winnin's get distributed to all da parishes. Da Awchdiocese is really hurtin', 'cause people ain't as holy as dey used to be."

This barrage of infomation was beyond the scope of Oleg's understanding. He could only concentrate on one fact.

"Charmaine, this sounds very good, my sign autograph. But is only one problem."

"What's dat?"

"I am not Catholic."

She smiled. "Aw, dat ain't a problem. We Catlicks let all kinds of Protestants in. We ain't gonna' bite. What are ya, Lutheran?"

"No," he said, hesitating. "I am Jew."

Charmaine gasped. "Really?" Her eyes grew wide, as though Oleg had just told her he was from Saturn, before she caught herself. "I beg your pawdon. It's just that I haven't met very many Jewish people before. Da last one, I think, was a girl named Ruthie Feldman who I met at summer camp back in eighth grade."

"Well, I am only Jew in name," he said. "I do not practice."

Charmaine laughed and waved him off. "Shoot, we don't really practice at bein' Catlicks. We're just really good at it." She thought for a moment. "Wait a second. Y'all da ones who don't celebrate Christmas, right?"

"We have our own celebration, very similar."

Charmaine rolled her lip in between her thumb and index finger, contemplating the revelation. "Wow. A Jew."

"Is big problem, yes?" Oleg looked grim.

Charmaine looked to her right, then to her left, checking to make sure no one was listening. "I'll tell you what," she said in barely a whisper. "It'll be our little secret."

Behind Oleg, Charmaine could hear the sound of a door opening and a pair of footsteps approaching on the wood floor.

"Oleg, ktory czy to?" a voice called out. A *woman's* voice. *"Ktora godzina?"* the woman said. Charmaine could make her out through the opening in the doorway. She was tall and beautiful with incredible cheekbones, wearing a bathrobe and drying her hair with a towel.

Panic filled Charmaine's heart, and she nearly turned to run back to her car before even saying goodbye. She had never even thought to ask if he was married. How could she have been so stupid!

Oleg turned quickly and called out behind him in a sharp voice. *"Chwileczke!"* He then turned back to face Charmaine, his eyes betraying no emotion. "Well, if is okay with you, I will help."

"Oh, right, okay," she said, almost forgetting for a moment her reason for coming. She began to back away, nearly tripping down the front stoop. "I'll tawk to ya later and give ya all the details. I gotta run if I'm gonna make it to my class on time." She brandished her key in her hand, ready to get the hell out of there.

***

Oleg, Robbie Gauthier, and snapper Frankie Phillips were camped out on the practice field at the 45-yard-line with a dozen footballs strewn about. Phillips grabbed a ball and shot it between his legs to Gauthier, who teed it up for Oleg to boot through the uprights, 65 yards away.

With a swift, thunderous motion that seemed effortless in its grace, Oleg blasted the ball the full distance, using just enough draw to hit dead center. "Was good, yes?" he said, expressionless.

"Looked good to me," Phillips said.

Gauthier squinted into the distance. "Think so. But I couldn't tell."

"What do you mean you couldn't tell?" Phillips said. "You got eyes, don't you?"

"We're about half a mile away," Gauthier said. "What, you think I'm like the Six-Million-Dollar Man with my telescopic vision?"

"More like half-million-dollar man," Phillips said, laughing as he grabbed another ball.

"Let us try from 40-yard-line," Oleg said.

"Okay, but don't ask Gauthier if it's good," Phillips said, moving into place for the snap.

"You got a lot of nerve, big boy," Gauthier said. "You can't even see your feet with that big gut of yours."

Before leaning over the ball, Phillips pointed to the clock on the sideline scoreboard. "Robbie, can you tell me what time it is?" he said, a sarcastic tone in his voice. "I don't want to miss lunch." He patted his belly.

Robbie squinted at the scoreboard, his aggravation mounting. "I dunno'. It's about 12, 12:15, something like that."

Phillips looked at Oleg and laughed. "Well, which is it? They do teach you how to tell time down on the bayou, don't they, Coonass?"

"Shut up and hike the ball," Gauthier said.

Phillips stared at his quarterback in disbelief, the realization setting in. "You're blind as a bat."

"I am not," Gauthier said.

"How'd you ever pass your physical?" Phillips said. "You need to get your eyes checked."

"Maybe that is why he throw so many pass to guy on other team," Oleg said.

Phillips burst into laughter. "Aw, 'Leg, that was below the belt. You better quit before you get your ass kicked."

Oleg smiled, enjoying the polite ribbing. "I am not scared. If I run far away, he cannot see."

"Just shut up and kick the damn ball," Gauthier said, putting an end to the discussion.

As he prepared to call the signal, Robbie got an idea. He turned to Oleg and said, "Say, 'Leg, they got Charlie Brown in Poland?"

Phillips couldn't help overhearing. He craned his neck back to comment. "Aw, no, man, don't do that. That ain't right."

Oleg was confused. "I am not familiar. Who is this Charlie Brown?"

"Oh, never mind," Gauthier said, winking at Phillips, who shook his head in resignation.

"Don't do it, Rob," Phillips said.

"Do what?" Oleg said.

"Nothing," Gauthier said. He dropped to one knee and held his hands out to catch the snap. Oleg marked off his distance from the holder and went through his pre-kick ritual.

"Down. Set. Hut. Hut," Gauthier barked.

Phillips fired the ball through his legs. Gauthier caught it, set it down, and with the most nimble of motions, removed it from the path of Oleg's foot. Time seemed to stand still, as Oleg swung his leg with the force of a Roman cata-pult. Finding no resistance, the leg's momentum carried Oleg upward and outward until his body levitated along a horizontal plane. He hung in the air a split-second before landing on the turf with a dull thud.

Even though he felt sorry for the poor schlub, Phillips couldn't resist laughing at the comical scene. It couldn't have worked more perfectly if Charles Schulz had drawn it himself. The escapade caught the attention of everyone around, and they whooped and hollered in derision, if only because a good humiliation would keep their star kicker's head from getting too big, what with all the attention he'd received in the last two weeks.

"Come on, buddy," Gauthier said. "Let me give you a hand there." He reached down to pull Oleg to his feet. As soon as Oleg had regained his footing, in a rare display of aggression, he lunged at Robbie and began to grapple like a Greco-Roman wrestler.

"What the hell?" Gauthier shouted, a smile on his face. Oleg struggled to wrap his arms around the 6-foot-4-inch quarterback's broad shoulders.

"'Leg, calm down, bud," Phillips said. "It was just a joke. No harm intended."

"No offense taken," Oleg said, a slight smile cracking through his clenched teeth.

"Hey, hey, there," Gauthier said. "Ease up, 'Leg. I don't want to have to use the 'Crawdad Crusher' on ya. You know my cousin Gator was in the WWF."

Oleg brushed aside the threat, having leapt upon Gauthier's back and threaded his arms around his neck and placed his hands over his eyes. Gauthier spun around in circles trying to dislodge his tormentor like a blindfolded bull trying to toss off a chimpanzee. After a minute, he realized that he was not only too dizzy to stand up, but there was no way for him to break Oleg's hold. Little by little, his defense folded.

"Okay, okay, I give," he said. "I give."

Once Gauthier had come to a stand-still, Oleg dropped back down to the ground and slapped his hands together to mimic wiping off dirt.

The only wound the strapping, young quarter-back had suffered was to his pride.

"What the heck was that voodoo grip you put on him?" Phillips said.

"I was wrestler in sport academy," Oleg said. "During winter, when not playing football. Was my favorite move, though never use on big guy before." He turned to Gauthier, who had leaned over and rested both hands on his knees. "Are you okay?"

Without answering, Gauthier placed his palms over his eyes, then removed them and blinked in an exaggerated fashion.

"Hey, big guy, everything okay?" Phillips said, a little concerned.

Still silent, Gauthier turned toward the

scoreboard, blinked again, and rubbed his eyes even harder.

"What?" Phillips said. "What is it?"

A wide grin spread across Robbie's face, and he nearly knocked Oleg to the ground trying to give him a big hug.

"I can see!"

***

When the Saints took the field in Philadelphia that Sunday, an uneducated observer might have thought they were the perennial NFC champs rather than the host Eagles.

Cedric once again ran with the power, speed, and ankle-breaking cutbacks that made him a threat to take it to the house on any given carry. Dexter once again displayed the dazzling speed and leaping ability that wowed scouts when he came out of Florida State a decade earlier. Oleg added his booming, unreturnable kickoffs and tacked on field goals of 28 and 48 yards.

And Robbie Gauthier, after bouncing around the AFL, the CFL, the WFL, and the NFL, finally lived up to his potential. Despite a shaky first quarter, the Cajun Cannon settled down and connected on 12 consecutive passes on his way to a 24-of-36 performance for 318 yards and four TDs – against the league's formerly No. 2-rated pass defense. On this day, the Saints made the reigning conference champs look like chumps.

Final score: Saints 34, Eagles 20.

Week 14
4 Wins, 8 Losses

Byron Fielding stared across his desk at
Minka Adamowicz, captivated by her devastating
cheekbones, the same facial features that had
propelled her to a career as a top fashion model
on the runways of New York, Paris, and Milan.

With her best years behind her, the lupine
vixen had set her sights on the business end of
the skin trade, carving out a healthy niche with
her own modeling agency, shuttling pretty, naive,
young girls over from Eastern Europe. Minka,
who dropped her cumbersome last name years
earlier, was well accustomed to dealing with male
pigs, and she was perfectly willing to use every
wile and charm to her advantage. The fool sitting
across the desk from her would be no match.

It didn't help matters that Fielding could
count on one hand the number of women he'd
ever known Biblically. The reluctant bachelor
suffered from a pathological lack of charisma
even in the presence of an average-looking

woman. Staring at Minka, he became a blithering idiot, Tulane MBA or no.

Coupled with Ron Beauchamp – who, even at his advanced age, chased every young hen that caught his eye and had the string of four failed marriages to progressively younger women to show for it – the duo were ill-equipped to deal with any female, whether a shrewd tactician like Governor Fontenot or a mercenary like Minka.

"So good to meet you in person," Fielding said. He nervously rearranged papers, pens, and photos on his desk in a frantic attempt to retain his composure. "It's good to finally put a face to the name."

"Yes, is good," Minka said, cocking her head at just the right angle to stare down her nose at her adversary. "Thank you for meeting me on a Saturday." Without breaking eye contact, she reached into her snakeskin handbag, produced a cigarette and lit up. The thought of asking for permission had not even occurred to her. "You are much younger and more...handsome than I had pictured." Blowing out a cloud of smoke, Minka flashed a coy smile.

"Well, I'm not *that* young." His voice cracking, Fielding cleared his throat and straightened his tie. "Ms. Adamowicz, I can assure you..."

"Please, call me Minka."

"Okay, Minka. Again, I can assure you that the situation with Oleg's paychecks, well, that was just an administrative error."

"Was not error," Minka said, tapping her ash into a coffee cup at the edge of the desk. She smiled again, this time as though she were privy to Fielding's secret. "I believe everything happen for reason."

"Well, uh, yes, uh, well, anyway, we should be able to get that straightened out right away, no problem." Fielding couldn't believe what was happening to him. He had negotiated multi-million-dollar deals for some of the league's biggest stars. He had stared down some of the league's sharpest super-agents without so much as a blink. But this woman was getting the better of him before the first move had even been made. Was that a drop of sweat running down his right temple?

"Do not bother," Minka said with a wave of her hand. She crossed one leg over the other and sat back in her chair, tilting her head upward to issue another blast of thick smoke into the air.

"What do you mean?"

"Is not necessary," she said.

"Well, Oleg does want his money, doesn't he? He'll need those checks signed if he wants to cash them."

"Yes, he wants money. But those checks, they are insult. Oleg wants new deal if he is to stay with Saint."

"New deal?"

"Oleg is currently making league minimum."

"Well, you're the one who negotiated his original contract," Fielding said.

"Yes, but that was before Oleg is number three scoring in league. Current contract is insult. We must support large family. Father in Poland is very old."

Fielding sensed a tingling on the left side of his face. This one was definitely a droplet of sweat. What to do? Sure, he had planned for a little niggling over the checks, but an all-out contract negotiation? And with a woman of such guile. Fielding needed to stall. He needed time to gather his thoughts, forge a gameplan.

"Ms. Adamowicz...Minka, I understand your concerns, but we're three-quarters of the way through this season. It's too late in the game to sign a new deal now. And to be perfectly honest, we don't have the money."

Minka leaned forward and mashed her butt out in the empty coffee cup, shooting smoke through a tiny gap in the corner of her mouth. Folding her arms, she sat upright and arched an eyebrow. "Is not what Atlanta Falcon said."

Fielding swallowed hard. "Excuse me?"

"Is team that called last week to talk with Oleg. You know Atlanta Falcon, yes?"

"Well, yes, they're our archriv...they're in our division. We know them well. You say you've spoken with them?"

"Yes, but I tell them we must honor contract with Saint." Minka had Fielding's full attention now. She toyed with him like a cat with a rubber mouse. "They say they want to take Oleg from Saint just like they did with Sven Gustafson. Want to do it just to...how you say...screw you."

The weight of Minka's words made Fielding nearly choke on his own saliva. As much as the recollection still haunted Saints fans, it haunted team management even more, because of the way the Falcons had swooped in during a contract renegotiation and inked the deal in less than 24 hours. Making matters worse, it had all occurred after a minor misunderstanding with the beloved Swedish-born kicker.

Fielding knew he couldn't let lightning strike twice. But given the organization's dire financial straits, he had little room to maneuver. And without Beauchamp's okay, he was powerless to act. He needed time, more time, but Minka kept turning the screw tighter.

"Would be shame if public find out Saint not pay star kicker. You think they will believe Mr. Beauchamp forgot to sign checks?" She gave Fielding a weak smile. "Public not as naive as my Oleg."

"Minka, are you trying to threaten me?"

"Is no threat. If Saint want to keep stadium deal alive, you will negotiate. Otherwise I will call *Daily Doubloon* to tell about paycheck, and then Atlanta Falcon to get Oleg new contract."

Clearly this woman knew much more than she let on. Fielding would have had to smile at her clever tactics if he weren't so desperate to find a way to stop the hemorrhaging. With his nimble mind pushed to the brink, the former Mathlete and champion debater resorted to desperate measures heretofore unimagineable. Drawing from a wellspring of confidence and charm the source of which he knew not, Byron Fielding took a deep breath and, before analysis paralysis could set in, he asked the beautiful woman sitting before him out on a date.

"Minka, I want to apologize for being so rude," he said. "I don't know how you do it in New York, but this is not the way we like to do business in New Orleans. Down here, it's perfectly acceptable to mix business with pleasure. Tell you what, why don't we discuss this over dinner and a bottle of wine, and we can put our heads together on this deal. What do you say?"

Though no less swayed, Minka was impressed by Fielding's agile recovery. After all, for her, it was the chase and not the kill that brought the most pleasure. She licked her chops hungrily.

"Sound good," she said, her eyes lighting up. "Pick me up at eight."

***

St. Peter Catholic Church was an austere, red-brick building of early-20th-century lineage plopped in the heart of Arabi, a working-class suburb downriver from the heart of the city.

With the white population dying out (or moving out) and replaced by blacks, most of whom were Protestants of one variety or another, the 90-year-old church parish had been teetering on the brink of collapse for several years.

That's why Father Joe Pastore viewed the overflow crowd at the 11 a.m. service as a minor miracle. He responded with his best homily in years, eschewing the tired dogma of Catholic hard-liners in an effort to connect viscerally with his audience. The message resonated perhaps most strongly with the guest of honor, who greeted his host in the church foyer after the Mass with a hearty handshake.

"Thank you for speech, Father," Oleg said. "Much wisdom in your words."

"Father Joe is known for his homilies," said Charmaine, who stood at Oleg's side, escorting him through the crowd.

"I appreciate the compliment, Oleg," Father Pastore said. "But I can't take credit. It's all from here." He tapped the Bible in his hand.

Oleg smiled and nodded toward the book. "Maybe I should try reading sometime."

"I'd be happy to give you a free Bible study class...long as you keep coming here for mass every week. This crowd is amazing."

"People look for truth with capital T," Oleg

said. "Sometimes find in religion. Sometimes in sport. Sometimes both."

"Lord knows I've said enough prayers watching the Saints play over the years," Father Pastore said. "You've been a godsend to the team. And your being here today sets a tremendous example." He draped his arm around Oleg's shoulder and lowered his voice. "Although I couldn't help noticing that you skipped communion. Is there something wrong? Something you'd like to talk about?"

Oleg shrugged. "Was not hungry."

Charmaine, who had leaned close to eavesdrop, laughed uneasily and tried to cover for her Jewish friend. "Father, you know how it is wit' at'letes on game day. He's gotta' be real careful wit' what he eats."

"Ah, I see," Father Pastore said. "Well, may the Lord give you energy in abundance today." He lifted his hand to make the sign of the cross in front of Oleg's face, but before he could finish, Charmaine had yanked Oleg out the front door.

Despite the powerful hurricane now looming ominously in the Gulf of Mexico, the sun shone brightly on this mild fall day. The St. Peter Women's Auxiliary, all four of them, had set up a cafeteria-style table out in front of the church for the autograph signing. Beside Oleg's spot on the table sat a shoebox for the donations. Manning the box was none other than Shirley Fontana,

Charmaine's mother, who had posted a sign on the table that read:

Donations Optional
(but it's a sin if you don't)

Once Oleg took his seat, the crowd began to file past in orderly fashion. Men, women, and children of all ages and backgrounds came prepared with items for Oleg to sign. Footballs, shirts, trading cards, football game programs, lingerie. Just about anything that would hold an ink signature and a few objects that wouldn't, such as one little boy's golden retriever.

Shirley Fontana possessed just the right balance of warmth and threatening menace to extract the most generous donations from each petitioner. And Father Joe would have been more than satisfied with his take on the day but for Crazy Maude Impastato, who sent the proceedings into another trajectory altogether.

Since the death of her husband, Vinnie, the 67-year-old widow had been afflicted with a laundry list of maladies that no doctor could ever detect or confirm. Speculation was that she did it for attention, especially since her three sons had left the neighborhood. Her behavior had grown so erratic that she had become not only a pariah but, essentially, a shut-in as well.

Seeing Crazy Maude at the front of the line, Shirley Fontana braced herself for the unexpected. The old woman leaned forward toward

Oleg and spoke softly, clutching her oversized purse against her chest.

"Is it true what they say about you?" she said, scratching behind her ear, uncontrollable itching being just one of her many tics.

"Excuse me?" Oleg said.

"Come on, Maude," Shirley Fontana said. "You want him to sign somethin' or what?"

Crazy Maude ignored Shirley and leaned closer. "Is it true you healed Robbie Gauthier?"

"Hey lady, speed it up," a young father called out from several spots back in the line.

"No. Is not true," Oleg said. "Was just coincidence."

"Robbie Gauthier wasn't blind," Charmaine said, hovering behind Oleg. "He's just dumb."

"Awright, Maude, let's go," Shirley said. "Ya holdin' up da line."

Crazy Maude grew desperate, and she reached out to seize Oleg's hand. "Please. Just touch my arm. Please, heal me."

"Now, Maude, ya makin' a scene," Shirley said. "Come on and let da man go."

"Momma, if you want me to jack her wit' my mace, just let me know," Charmaine said.

Father Pastore noticed the commotion, and he moved to the edge of the table.

"Is there something I can help with?" he said.

"Please," Maude said, near tears. Relinquishing her grip on Oleg, she plunged her hand into

her purse and pulled out a wad of cash. "Please
help me. I'll pay. Anything. Please."

The crumpled hundred-dollar-bills caught
Father Pastore's attention, and he nodded ap-
provingly, first to Shirley, then to Oleg. As if to
assist in the process, the priest grabbed Oleg by
the forearm and yanked it across the table,
simultaneously pushing Crazy Maude forward so
that Oleg's hand cupped the woman's forehead.

Oleg seemed like a passive observer to the
act, and he was as startled as anyone by the
result: A peaceful smile slowly washed over
Crazy Maude's face, her scratching subsided,
and like a cripple at a pentecostal revival, she
screamed for all to hear.

"I'm healed!"

With that grand pronouncement, those
gathered began scrounging in their wallets for
more cash, hoping to be cured of afflictions large
and small, real and imagined. Something so
trivial as an autograph dwindled in significance
by comparison. Men sought relief for their acid
reflux. Women for their bunions. Children for
tonsilitis. Eczema, impotence, hypertension, heart
disease, cataracts, colitis, and even The Big C –
everything was in play.

Cell phones fired up to alert friends, family,
and neighbors of the events unfolding. What had
originally been planned as an hour-long autograph session turned into a marathon testimony

to the power of faith.

Much as he wanted to protest, Oleg did not
have the heart to deny the petitions, not when the
effects, both tangible and abstract, were so
readily apparent. And then there was the cash.

When it seemed that Shirley Fontana's
shoebox couldn't hold any more money, a taxicab
pulled up at curbside and a tall, beautiful woman
jostled her way to the front of the line. Minka.

"Oh Gawd, dat's his wife," Charmaine said
to her mother, ducking down behind her in a
futile attempt to hide.

"Shame on you, takin' up with a married
man," Shirley said in a scolding whisper. "You
need to get Father Joe to hear your confession
right now."

"But Mom, I didn't know he was married."

With no regard for the others in line, Minka
commanded Oleg's attention.

"We must talk," she said.

Oleg pointed to the people waiting patiently
in the long line. "You can see line, yes?"

"Forget line," Minka said with a dismissive
wave. "This is important."

Oleg sat back and crossed his arms. "So
important you do not come home last night?"

"You see what ya did," Shirley Fontana
whispered to her daughter. "Dey in a quarrel
'cause of you, ya little Jezebel."

"Shhhhh," Charmaine said.

"Do not worry," Minka said. "Was renegoti-
ating your contract. You will be very happy."

"Negotiating contract all night long?"

"Was tough negotiation." Minka reached into
her purse and tapped out a cigarette. Lighting up,
she blew out a long stream of smoke and recalled
the ordeal as would a conquering warrior. "But
in the end I broke him like a twig. Make Fielding
beg for mercy."

"What do you mean?" Oleg said.

"Fielding give good deal. You will be able to
buy house for Father."

"For me?" said Father Pastore, who had also
grown intrigued by the mysterious woman.

"For father in Poland," Oleg said.

"Oh," the priest said, mildly disappointed.

"Will get 5.2 million," Minka said.

"What is 5.2 million?" Oleg said.

"Is new contract from Saint. You will get 5.2
million dollars starting next year."

"5.2 million dollars!" Charmaine said,
shooting up like a Jack in the Box.

"Shhhhh," Shirley said.

"Who is this?" Minka said.

"Is my friend Charmaine," Oleg said. "Why?
You have problem?" Minka sized her up like a
side of beef.

Shirley tugged on her daughter's arm. "You
betta' apologize now while you can. I don't want
anotha' catfight in front of da church."

"Please Mrs. Adamowicz, I didn't know dat Oleg was married," Charmaine said. "I hope you'll forgive me."

"Married? What are you talking about?" Minka threw back her head and laughed. "I am not Oleg wife. I am sister."

***

In stark contrast to the Saints' recent surge, the Minnesota Vikings were suffering from yet another late-season swoon under quarterback D'Andre Mulberry. With the ESPN Sunday night crew in the Dome televising the game to a national audience, the two teams presented a study in vastly differing fortunes.

On the second play from scrimmage, Mulberry tripped on his own untied shoelace and sprained his ankle. This wouldn't have been so bad, except that he'd also forgotten to button his chinstrap. Defensive tackle Ezekiel Robinson's flexi-cast caught him with a right uppercut, knocking Mulberry unconscious and simultaneously breaking his jaw. Backup quarterback Sean McMahon proceeded to throw five – yes, five – interceptions, thus confirming his status as a bust after finishing second in the Heisman voting during his senior year of college.

The Vikes tacked on two fumbles, and the rout was on. The Saints led 27-10 at halftime on their way to a 41-17 drubbing.

It would have been a ho-hum victory except

for one curious incident midway through the third quarter. After Robinson appeared to blow out his ACL on the dome's new turf and was carted into the locker room, several players were seen huddling around Oleg in a heated discussion.

Moments later, Robinson returned to the sidelines, where Oleg appeared to administer some type of deep-tissue massage to Robinson's injured knee. Before the quarter had ended, Robinson had not only returned to the lineup, he went on to finish the game, recording 12 tackles and two sacks.

Week 15
5 Wins, 8 Losses

"Next caller on da line, we got my man, Rip, from Chalmette. What'cha say, Rip?"

"Hey, Lonnie, how ya doin'? I was jus' wonderin', what'cha think about dis hurricane in da Gulf? You think it's gonna' be da big one like everybody's talkin' 'bout?"

Lonnie Benedetto paused and took a gulp of his lukewarm coffee sitting on the table of his makeshift broadcast booth inside Hurrah's Casino at the foot of Canal Street. Barely an hour into his nightly call-in show, his patience was already wearing thin.

"Rip, all dese years I been on TV and on da radio," Lonnie said, with just a hint of sarcasm in his voice, "you ever seen me do da weather?"

"Uhh, no, Lonnie, I can't say as I have."

"Well, then what da heck ya aksin' me about da weather for? You wanna' know about dis hurricane, go aks Nash Roberts. Next caller."

"Say Lonnie," a woman's voice said over the

line. She sounded a bit shaky from nerves. "First-time, long-time, ain't dat what dey say?"

"Yeah, Dawlin'," Lonnie said, warming to his guest. "Take ya time. Don't be nervous. Now what'cha say?"

The woman took an audible breath. "Well, my cousin's hairdresser told her she heard dat Ron Beauchamp was holdin' out on payin' Oleg 'cause he's been badmouthin' him in da press. Den he was tryin' to cut Oleg 'cause he was demandin' a new contract."

Lonnie smiled, given the opportunity to launch into his favorite topic – bashing the Saints. To be fair, Lonnie loved the Saints perhaps more than anyone else in town. He'd covered the team since day one and stuck with them through thick and thin. But in light of his Sicilian roots, Lonnie B just couldn't keep his mouth shut when he saw something he didn't agree with. And considering the team's history of questionable management decisions, his mouth was open a lot.

"Dawlin', I heard dat same rumor," Lonnie said. "But I haven't been able to confirm it. If ya aks me, though, it sounds right in character for Beauchamp an' dat bunch of squirrels."

Lonnie B had long since fallen out of favor with the Saints' owner. He'd been kicked off the team plane, kicked off the team bus, kicked out of the team locker room. About the only thing that hadn't been kicked yet was the bucket, and Lonnie was holding fast at age 75 despite a ticker that skipped a beat once in a while, especially whenever he drew a straight flush at his favorite Hurrah's poker table.

"First dey wanna' shake down da governor for a new stadium," the caller said. "Now dey wanna' shake down their best player. It's a cryin' shame, if ya aks me."

"When's Beauchamp gonna' learn?" Lonnie said. "Dat dog won't hunt around here, especially wit' Governor Fontenot. Pawdon my French, but I hear dat woman's a real ball-breaker."

Despite more than 30 years on the air, Lonnie B had never succumbed to the conventions of the American broadcasting industry. Instead, he continually practiced and nearly perfected the lazy tongue and colorful expressions he'd grown up with on North Salcedo Street. Now, with a new set of dentures, he didn't just grapple with the English language on a daily basis. He body-slammed it, put it in a sleeper-hold, and squeezed it into submission – a trait that endeared him all the more to his loyal fans, who seemed to revel in and relish each and every slip of the tongue.

"We got another caller on da line," Lonnie said, "and this is a real surprise. It's none other than Governor Fontenot herself. What'cha say, Governor? I hope you're not offended 'cause I called you a..."

"Not at all, Lonnie, not at all," Fontenot said. "Coming from a straight-shooter like you, I take it as a compliment."

The 56-year-old former schoolteacher and mother of four conducted herself with the gracious air of a polished politician. Having risen through the ranks of state government, from State Representative to State Senator to Secretary of State to Lieutenant Governor, she had now reached the pinnacle of Louisiana politics, a first for any woman in the state's history.

"I know this is a sports show," she said, "but I wanted to talk directly to your audience and urge them to seek shelter from Hurricane Ronald, which has just been upgraded to a Category 3 storm with winds over 111 miles per hour. It's projected to make landfall in the next 36 to 48 hours, and we're urging everyone along coastal Louisiana to evacuate to higher ground. Most importantly, if, for some reason, you're not in a position to leave town, we're opening up the Louisiana Superdome as a public shelter."

Seizing the opportunity, Lonnie tried to steer the conversation back to sports. "Thank you for that important announcement, Governor. Does your decision to open the Dome as a public shelter have any bearing on your current talks with Ron Beauchamp and the Saints?"

"Absolutely not. Quite simply, the Louisiana Superdome is the largest publicly owned structure in metropolitan New Orleans and the most suitable venue to use for this emergency."

"Well since I got ya on the line, can you tell us how the negotiations are going?"

"We've made our case very clearly. I won't allow the interests of a few greedy men be placed before the interests of the people of Louisiana."

"Are you willing to put your position as governor on the line over this?" Lonnie said. "How will you feel if you go down in history as the governor who let the Saints leave?"

"The State of Louisiana has many other problems more significant than a football team. Education. Healthcare. Jobs. These are the issues that matter most to voters. If keeping this team means our elementary schools won't have new textbooks or our state highways won't be improved, then that's a deal I won't make. If losing this team means that we will have the funds to provide medical care for sick children, then my conscience will be clear. At the end of the day, I have to remember that the people of Louisiana elected me to serve the needs of this great state...not to run a football team."

Lonnie chuckled heartily, knowing he'd stirred the pot and elicited the kind of juicy sound-bite that would be repeated on news shows around the state for the next week. "Remember folks, you heard it here foist," Lonnie said. "Governor Fontenot, thank you for coming on the show tonight. And to those of you in low-lying areas, take cover. Hurricane Ron's on its way."

                    ***

Opening the Dome as a public shelter seemed like a good idea initially. But it was only a matter of time before the 25,000 or so storm refugees began causing trouble, considering they had nothing to do, nowhere else to go and inadequate Dome staffing or security to provide proper oversight – which was just fine with Ron Beauchamp. Any physical damage to the stadium, whether internal or external, added fuel to his argument for a new one.

With Hurricane Ronald bearing down on the Louisiana coastline packing sustained winds of 125 miles per hour, Mayor Cyril Bartholomew had issued an evacuation order to all who could get out and imposed a curfew on all those who couldn't. State Police had redirected traffic flow on all major arteries, creating an outbound, six-lane convoy to higher ground extending as far as the eye could see. Unofficial estimates ranged from 500,000 to 1 million residents leaving the region to stay with nearby family or wait it out in hotel rooms, which were booked solid as far west as Houston and as far north as Memphis.

Many of those left behind barricaded themselves in their homes, hoping to ride out what was predicted to be the "doomsday" storm that New Orleanians had awaited since Betsy in 1965 left the city underwater for a week. The rest headed for the Dome.

Among those were Oleg and Minka, who had no family or friends in the area nor the means of evacuating, after politely declining an offer from Charmaine and the Fontana clan to accompany them to an uncle's house in Dallas.

Given Beauchamp's money woes, he had chosen to keep his football team in New Orleans to practice in the Dome rather than charter a plane and rent out temporary facilities in a safe location such as San Antonio or Little Rock. The decision incited outright mutiny, led by Jake Radke himself, who attempted to relocate practice to his dude ranch in New Mexico. And while a handful of players followed dutifully, most scattered to the wind, eager to enjoy a couple of rare late-season days off.

Not that anyone was particularly worried about the week's opponent. At 3-and-10, the hapless Arizona Cardinals were practiced in the art of self-mortification and one of the few teams in the league with a history of futility to rival the Saints. Besides, even with their 5-game winning streak, the Saints would need a small miracle just to have an outside chance of making the playoffs.

For his part, Beauchamp had no room to grouse, having escaped to his hunting cabin in Arkansas. Fielding also fled, to Miami of all places, to care for his elderly mother. But as a

gesture of affection toward Minka, he had given
her the key to the Owner's Suite, which is where
she and her brother found themselves, watching
from the suite's balcony an impromptu touch
football game played by storm refugees on the
Dome's QuikTurf.

"Savages," Minka said, watching a player on
the field disregard the rules and take down an
opposing ball-carrier with a vicious hit.

"Is America's sport," Oleg said, holding an
eight-inch shrimp po-boy in one hand and a cold
beer in the other. He had raided the suite's fridge,
which was still loaded with top-notch grub from
the previous game day. "Football is more popular
than baseball now."

"Football like America itself." Minka tapped
a cigarette out of her slim, gold case, lit up and
blew a train of smoke into the recirculated air.

"How do you mean?" Oleg said.

"Fast...powerful...brutal." Without a thought,
Minka tossed her match down onto a crowd of
people below who were ripping cushions from the
Dome seating and building some sort of pyre.

"You have been in New York too long."

"Football is no different than modeling,"
Minka said. "They treat you like piece of meat.
Must get all you can now before they toss you
out on sidewalk like trash."

Oleg shook his head, recognizing the familiar
road this conversation with his sister was taking.

"Is beautiful game, really. Speed. Power. Grace. Intellect. Is like symphony."

"Ha!" Minka had to laugh, observing as the game on the field turned into an all-out streetfight right on top of the Saints logo at midfield. A knock on the door caught their attention. Oleg went to answer it and found a young black man.

"Say, dude, y'all got any more matches?" he said. "We tryin' to build us a lil' fire, 'cause it's cold all up in here."

"Uh, yes, here," Oleg said, finding a collection of New Orleans Saints matchbooks in an ashtray atop the counter of the kitchenette.

"Thank you," the man said, his eyes gravitating toward Oleg's sandwich. "Say, y'all ain't got no more them po-boys, do you? They was givin' away hot dogs, but they already ran out."

Without hesitating, Oleg handed the man his sandwich. "Here. We have many more sandwich in refrigerator anyway."

"Yeahyouright," the man said, wrapping his hand around the po-boy. "Thank you, sir. Y'all have a good evening now."

Oleg fished another sandwich from the fridge and returned to the balcony.

"I hope you have locked door," Minka said. "He may come back with gun, try to rob us."

Oleg groaned. "You have become just like other Americans. Afraid of anyone not like you. Want to lock yourself in big, fancy house for protection. Think money will solve problems."

An incredulous look swept across Minka's face, and she mashed her cigarette out on the balcony floor. "You are such idiot. You act like a monk, but you are no different from rest. If you don't think money will solve problem, tell me, why do you want to buy house for Father?"

Oleg started to respond but couldn't. He tried again but caught himself halfway through his first word. Finally, he spoke in a low voice. "Just want him to be happy."

"He does not care about house. You know how he is. Father lives in different world. I think this is not about him. Is about you."

"I am not the one who close door on son."

"Because you will not accept who you are. You are Jew, like me, like Father, like all who are persecuted for their faith."

"But I cannot accept what I do not believe."

Minka had no patience for her brother's insolence. "You don't believe in Holocaust?" she fired back. "You don't believe in Auschwitz?"

"I do not believe in religion as reason for killing. Do not believe in ordinary men who put words in book. Do not believe in empty rules."

"What do you believe?"

"I believe in spirit. Spirit is all."

"Please, Oleg, it only takes little gesture to please him. Just go to Temple. Act like you care."

"Would be dishonest. Would be blasphemy."

Minka rolled her eyes. "You may fool others, but you don't fool me. You are coward."

"That is ridiculous."

"Act like possession mean nothing to you."

"But they don't."

"Is not because you are pious. Is because you are afraid of attachment. Protect you from pain. You shut out world. Act like robot."

"Is not about possessions. Is about truth in soul, something you would not know about."

"I know one thing," Minka said. "Even soul cannot live alone. Need others to survive. Need love. Need hope. Why do you think New Orlyuns people treat you like holy man?"

"These people are blind."

"But you are their hero. They think you are Superman."

Oleg winced. "I am normal. Is nothing special about me. They are just little crazy, is all."

Minka shook her head, seeing she was getting nowhere. "Is like in modeling..."

"To you, everything like modeling."

"In modeling, people always look for next big thing. These people, they want something new to help them believe. If you have what they want, why not give it to them?"

"Because they could find it inside themselves ...if they looked," Oleg said. "To pretend other-wise would be a lie." His face contorted in revulsion as he spit out the words.

Another knock at the door broke through the long, uncomfortable silence, and despite a stern look from Minka, Oleg went to answer it. Minka looked over his shoulder and was frightened to see not only the black man who'd visited earlier but also a pack of his rough-hewn cohorts and several dirty-faced children.

"Say man, I know you said you had more po-boys. You think you got any to spare for these muhfuggas here? We hungry."

Despite a sharp pinch from his sister in the small of his back, Oleg threw the door open to the unwashed horde and invited them all inside. Within seconds, the entire suite was filled beyond capacity, and Oleg was handing out sandwiches as fast as he could retrieve them from the refrigerator. It seemed the caterers had left enough food to feed a small army. For every sandwich taken, another appeared. Which was fortunate, because Oleg couldn't bear to turn anyone away.

"'Leg, that you?" a man's voice called out amid the clamor.

Oleg met eyes with a middle-aged black man and smiled, "Mister Leroy, how are you?"

Leroy hooted with delight. "Shoulda' known you'd be up in the VIP suite." He turned to the others to explain. "'Leg stay next door to me on Miro Street. Me and him homeboys. Ain't that right, 'Leg?"

Oleg nodded in assent while handing a roast

beef and swiss to his friend.

"It's time to turn this mutha' out," Leroy said. "They got any Crown Royal up in here? We gon' get this bitch crunk!"

From that point, what could have been an unbearable situation mutated into an all-out party to rival Harry Connick Jr.'s annual Orpheus Mardi Gras extravaganza. The kicker (literally) occurred when Leroy convinced Oleg to put on a kicking exhibition down on the field.

Oleg entertained the crowd with displays of ball juggling (from his soccer days) and field-goal kicking that would become the stuff of legend. Urged on by the raucous crowd, he attempted progressively longer kicks, while the onlookers placed wagers on the outcome of each attempt. After a few, routine warm-up kicks from 45 and 50 yards, Oleg quickly found his rhythm and connected from 60 and 70 yards using a traditional hold. But when pressed to go even longer, Oleg opted for the unorthodox: he employed a drop-kicking technique he'd developed in Europe for soccer.

By releasing the potential energy supplied to the ball from its bounce off the ground, Oleg had learned that he could kick a ball 20 percent farther. Having consulted the NFL rulebook before his trans-Atlantic voyage and found this to be allowed in American football, he had been waiting for just the right opportunity to unveil his new method. The results were immediately evident to all in attendance that day, as he easily nailed kicks from 80 and 85 yards. For the record, either would have been good from 90.

***

The real story of Week 15 in New Orleans was not the Saints' 31-13 demolition of the Cardinals. It wasn't Oleg's remarkable 73-yard field goal in the closing seconds of the first half, using his innovative drop-kicking technique, which was proven to be legal after a coach's challenge prompted consultation of the rulebook. It wasn't even that Hurricane Ronald had skirted the Louisiana coast and made landfall in Biloxi, Mississippi, wreaking havoc on that booming Gulf Coast town. No, the real story was the utter destruction that had occurred *inside* the Dome from the unruly mob held captive for 36 hours.

Entire sections of seating had been torched, concession stands looted, and luxury suites vandalized, all in a quest by storm refugees to provide for basic necessities. The prevailing sentiment among them was one of anger toward city officials, state officials, Dome officials – toward anyone – at the lack of preparation, the woefully inadequate provisions, the inhumane nature in which so many had been corralled and expected to remain quietly for so long. Had it not been for Oleg's small gesture, suffice it to say the situation would have been much, much worse.

Week 16
6 Wins, 8 Losses

BILOXI, Mississippi – Cleanup continued in this Gulf Coast city in the aftermath of Hurricane Ronald, as residents and business owners attempted to pick up the pieces of their lives scattered to the wind by the powerful storm.

But authorities are breathing a sigh of relief after Ronald weakened in the final hours before moving ashore. Despite three persons dead in Mississippi and preliminary damage estimates topping $120 million along the Gulf Coast, many are thankful, knowing the situation could have been much, much worse.

Two-thirds of losses from the storm occurred in the Gulfport-Biloxi metropolitan area, which was hit dead-on by the storm's 100 mile-per-hour winds last Wednesday. The most glaring example of destruction was the Beau Maison Resort & Casino, which had been near completion when the storm struck.

According to eyewitnesses who rode the

storm out in the neighboring Tropical Isle
Casino, high winds ripped the roofs from several
Beau Maison structures, allowing rain and salt
water from the accompanying storm surge to
drench the interior of the buildings. The casino's
main gaming area suffered extensive damage, as
did nearly all of the resort's 600 hotel rooms.

"All gone," said Beau Maison owner Ronald
Beauchamp, who was visibly shaken upon seeing
the damage. "Game over. I'm finished."

Beauchamp said he'd hoped the new resort
and casino would help shore up his ailing housing development business, which had been reeling
after a series of earlier hurricanes ripped through
Beau Maison communities along the Gulf Coast.

"Back to the drawing board," he said.

Surveying the wreckage at the Beau Maison
site, one Hancock County Sheriff's Deputy
suggested the storm may have spawned a tor-
nado, which would account for the severity of the
damage and the peculiar, isolated path in which it
occurred. A cleanup worker, who asked not to be
identified, said the damage was due to the poor
quality of Beau Maison's construction.

None of the other 17 gaming establishments
along the stretch of Highway 90 between
Gulfport and Biloxi suffered substantial damage. By Friday, casino row had returned to life,
and those operations that survived the hurricane
reported brisk business.

***

"It's global warmin'," said Shirley Fontana, sitting in her Arabi home packed with family and friends for a holiday gathering. "How else ya gonna' explain a hurricane in mid-December?"

That Hurricane Ronald had occurred a full two weeks after the official close of the Atlantic hurricane season was a first for the record books. That a killer storm had, once again, skirted around New Orleans, sparing the city from certain destruction, had become commonplace.

"You ain't kiddin', Shirl," said her sister-in-law, Connie Fontana. "I'm still runnin' my air conditioner in my house. I mean, I didn't even get da Twinnies to put up my Christmas tree till after we got back from evacuatin'."

"It's the Lord's will," said an elderly woman cloaked in a nun's habit.

"Ain't dat da truth, Sista Mary Margaret," Shirley said.

"We jus' lucky we got da convent down in da Quarta'," Anthony Joseph "A.J." Fontana said upon entering the living room of the family shotgun, carrying a tray of mini-muffalettas. His thick black hair was slicked back, and he wore a red-checkered apron that barely covered his round belly. "Dem Ursuline nuns are like a force field around Nooawlins."

"Oh, you're right about dat, sugah," Connie said, acknowledging the 200-year-old convent on

Ursulines Street in the lower French Quarter.
Legend held that every time a hurricane threat-
ened the city, the nuns gathered for a marathon
prayer vigil until the threat passed. While any
number of meteorological explanations could be
found from storm to storm, a careful examination
of the city's history revealed an uncanny knack
for staving off the doomsday scenarios that many
had been predicting for the past 50 years.

Sister Mary Margaret bowed her head in
humility. "We do the Lord's work. That is all."

"Y'all need to say some prayers for da
Saints," Shirley said, cramming a mini-muff into
her mouth. "Dey win their last two games, dey
might still have a shot at da playoffs."

"Aww, Shirl, why ya wanna' go gettin' ya
hopes up?" A.J. said. "Same thing's gonna'
happen like always. Dey gonna' find some kinda'
way to snatch defeat from da jaws of victory."

"A.J., you jus' like all dese other pessimists
around here," Shirley said. "Ya been down so
long, ya forgot how to think positive. Not like da
Sistas here. Whadda' ya say, Sista?"

"Come on, Shirl," Connie said. "You can't
put da Sista on da spot like dat."

"Why not?" Shirley said. "Ya got a team
named da Saints. Ya got da Ursuline nuns prayin'
for 'em. And ya got a Jesus-look-alike kickin' for
'em. Da Dallas Cowboys might be America's
team. But da Saints are God's team."

A stern look washed over Sister Mary Margaret's face, and she wagged her index finger toward Shirley. "Remember, child, it is not right to take the Lord's name in vain."

Shirley grew penitent and drooped her shoulders. "I'm sorry, Sista. It's jus' dat, you know, God's gotta' throw us a bone sometime. It's hard work down here. Know what I mean?"

"Bless you, my child," Sister said, making the sign of the cross. A knock on the door interrupted her ministrations. A.J. rose to answer it.

"Father Joe," he said, welcoming the parish priest into the home. "What a pleasant surprise."

"I'm sorry to interrupt," Father Pastore said, "but I wanted to deliver this right away. I remembered you said Oleg was going to be here."

"Yeah, he's inna' back wit' Charmaine and da Twinnies," A.J. said. "Come in and join us. Can I get you anything? A muffaletta? Some wine?"

"Oh no thanks, I can't stay long. I have to get over to the community food pantry to help out."

"Hold on a sec, Father," Shirley said, struggling to her feet, before issuing a piercing shriek that echoed down the home's long hallway: "Shawwwwmaine! Alex! Ya got a visita'."

***

Charmaine and Oleg sat awkwardly on the bed in her old room while her two burly twin cousins, D.J. and E.J. (aka "The Twinnies"), modeled their latest get-rich-quick scheme:

oversized black vinyl bags with a zipper running up the middle and holes cut for the eyes, nose, mouth, arms, and feet.

Oleg sat impassive, thoroughly flummoxed by the fashion statement. "I do not understand."

Simultaneously, the Twinnies unzipped their bags and poked their heads out.

"Dude," D.J. said. "Think about it."

"We takin' da Baghead concept to a whole 'nother level," E.J. said.

Charmaine and Oleg stared blankly.

The Twinnies exchanged exasperated looks at their audience's mental lethargy.

"Bodybags," they blurted out in unison.

"For wearin' at da Saints games," D.J. said.

"Beats da hell outta' wearin' a freakin' paper bag on ya head," E.J. said. "Dis thing has class."

"And style," D.J. said. "We can get these at Morgue Mart for like a dollar and sell 'em for ten. We'll make a mint."

"Twinnies, y'all a trip," Charmaine said.

Oleg was still trying to grasp the concept. "Is bag for putting dead bodies? You think people will wear? Seems little creepy to me."

"Get real, 'Leg," D.J. said. "Dis is Noo-awlins. Jus' las' week, I seen a middle-age lady walkin' down Bourbon Street wearin' a styro-foam penis strapped to her forehead."

"No lie," E.J. said. "Dis past Mardi Gras, at da Krewe of Bacchus, I seen a dude dressed just like Britney Spears. Man, was he hot."

"Some people will wear anything to get into da spirit of it," D.J. said.

"Mardi Gras. Jazz Fest. Sugah Bowl. Like dey say, '*Lazy la baton roulette*,'" E.J. said.

"*Roulez*, ya moron," Charmaine said.

"Aw, you get my point," E.J. said. "Have ya noticed the getups some of dese fans wear? Like dat dude who dresses up like Moses?"

"Once word of dis hits, we won't be able to keep up wit' demand," D.J. said.

"But Twinnies, da Saints only got two more games left, and one of 'em's away."

D.J. and E.J.'s faces froze. How could they have overlooked such a key component of their business plan? E.J., being a full six minutes older than his brother and thus the more mature and intelligent of the pair, rebounded with an admirably positive outlook.

"You can consider it our test market," he said. "Dat'll give us a whole year to gear up for next season."

"If there is a next season," D.J. said.

"Dat way, we can see about gettin' a patent for our invention," E.J. said.

"You can't patent a bodybag," Charmaine said. "Dey awready done dat awready."

"You can too," E.J. said. "Long as it's for a new use. We ain't makin' da same mistake our father made, God rest his soul."

D.J., E.J., and Charmaine promptly bowed their heads and made the sign of the cross.

"What mistake?" Oleg said.

"My Uncle C.J. was da original Baghead," Charmaine said. "He invented it."

"He invented paper bag?" Oleg said.

"Nahh," E.J. said. "Ya see, he was a regular at da bar Lonnie B owns out on Metairie Road."

"But I thought Lonnie B was radio man," Oleg said.

"He is," E.J. said, "but he's a renaissance man, and da bar is like his own private club-house. So da story goes, since my dad was in da bag half da time, especially on gameday, one time he passed out on da bar before dey even left for da Dome, and his buddies put a paper bag on his head and drew a little face on it."

"Dis was during da Saints one-and-fifteen season back in 1981," D.J. said. "And it jus' so happened dat da camera kept cuttin' to him in da stands, and da announcers thought it was a riot. Well, Lonnie B, not wantin' to miss out on an opportunity, went on TV later dat night and did his entire sportscast wearin' dat very same bag. From dat point on, he took all da credit."

"Pop never even realized what happened," E.J. said. "By da time he did, it was too late."

"So Mister Lonnie B, he became rich from bag, yes?" Oleg said, trying to put the pieces together. The Twinnies looked at each other.

"Well, no," D.J. said. "But he coulda'. Dat's why we can't let thunder strike twice."

"Lightinin', ya idiot," E.J. said.

"What?"

"Lightinin'," Charmaine said.

"Nah, dat ain't lighnin'," D.J. said. "I think it's ya momma callin'. Dat lady's got a voice like a freakin' air horn."

***

The entourage filed into the front room one by one – Charmaine, Oleg, and The Twinnies, still wearing their ridiculous home-made smocks.

"There y'all are," Shirley said. "Alex, Father Joe is here to see ya. Says he's got somethin' special to give to ya. How 'bout dat."

Oleg stepped forward to greet the priest. "Good evening, Father," he said. "Nice to see you again."

"Oleg, the pleasure is all mine," Father Pastore said. "I wanted to come over right away and get this to you as fast as I could." He reached inside his black wool coat and produced an ornate papyrus envelope decorated with gold filigree and fastened by an oversized wax seal. He held the envelope as if it were a precious commodity.

"In recognition of the remarkable work you've done on behalf of the church," Father Pastore said, "I have a special dispensation for you from Pope Pius himself."

"The Pope!" Shirley said, feeling faint.

Gasps and cries of amazement filled the room. Everyone seemed overcome by the magnitude of the gesture, except for Oleg. Father's hand trembled as he offered the envelope.

"I've been told that His Holiness has become quite a fan of American football," Father Pastore said, "and the Saints are his favorite team."

"And I bet I can guess who da Pope's favorite playa' is," Shirley said.

"Thank you, Father," Oleg said modestly.

"Well, don't just stand there," Charmaine said. "Open it awready."

"Yeah, da suspense is killin' us," Shirley said, wiping the perspiration from her brow. In the interim, Sister Mary Margaret had produced a rosary and begun reciting prayers.

"How I wish my dear Carlo coulda' lived to see dis," Connie said, snatching Shirley's hankie and wiping a tear from her eye. "An honest-to-God saint, right here in our midst."

Oleg peeled open the envelope and pulled out the letter inside, holding it close to his eyes to read, while Charmaine and the Twinnies peered over his shoulder.

"What's it say?" A.J. said.

Oleg frowned. "I cannot read. I believe is written in Latin. Father, can you help?"

He handed the letter to the priest, who slipped on his reading glasses.

"Pius Pontificus, servus servorum dei dilecto filio Oleg Adamowicz, diocesei Novum Orleanorum, Salutem..."

"Pope Pius, Servant of the Servants of God, to my beloved son Oleg Adamowicz, of the diocese of New Orleans, Greetings."

Everyone in the room gasped again, even louder, at the personal letter from the Pope. Father continued his translation, speaking in halting English as he went.

"The Church recognizes the zeal of your religious life...and the repute of your conduct... and other praise-worthy merits of goodness and virtuousness...in regard to which you are commended to Us."

Shirley took a gulp of her wine and began fanning herself with her napkin. She then sneered at Sister Mary Margaret as if to say "top that."

Father continued. "By faithful and worthy testimony...induce us...to bestow you with spiritual favors and graces...That is why We, with gracious good-will in consideration of your above-mentioned merits, wish to grant you... permission to engage in physical labor...and refrain from fasting and abstinence...on Sunday, the Lord's Day."

Father lowered the letter and snickered.

"What is it, Father?" Shirley said.

"Yeah, what's so funny," Connie said.

"He's giving Oleg permission to play football

on Sundays with absolution from sin."

"You mean you need a special dispensation just to play football on Sundays?" A.J. said.

"Technically, it is the Lord's day," Father Joe said, "and as such, one is required to abstain from physical labor."

"Hmm. Guess I thought dat went out wit' da Blue Law," A.J. said.

"Well," Father Joe said with a wry smile, "we do have some flexibility in these matters, as you can see."

The women in the room let out a collective sigh of relief.

"Ya hear dat, Alex," Shirley said. "Ya not gonna' burn in hell."

"Hallelujah," Connie said.

Father Joe's smile dissolved. "But you're still required to attend mass, of course."

"Well, of course," Sister Mary Margaret said, crossing her arms and nodding in agreement.

The flurry of activity and attention was too much for Oleg to take. A pained expresssion covered his face, and he struggled to find the proper words.

"Aw, look, he's overcome wit' emotion," Shirley said. "He's gonna' cry."

"It's okay, son," A.J. said, draping an arm over Oleg's shoulder. "You're among family."

Despite the multitude of thoughts bouncing inside his head, only one prevailed. Oleg resolved to end the charade once and for all.

"Thank you, Father," he said. "Letter from Pope is thoughtful gesture. Am glad I will not rot in hell." This drew a laugh from everyone, breaking the solemnity of the mood. "But is only one problem."

"What's that, my son," Father Pastore said.

"I cannot hide truth any more," Oleg said.

"Oleg, no," Charmaine said, sensing the revelation about to come from his lips.

"What is it, Alex?" Shirley said.

"I am not Catholic," he said.

Father Joe smiled, relieved. "Oh, bless you, son, but that's nothing to apologize for."

Oleg remained distraught. "No. You do not understand. I am not even Christian."

Gasps of shock, still louder than any before, filled the room.

Father struggled to glean his meaning. "Son, what is it you're trying to say?"

Oleg swallowed hard before announcing for all to hear. "I am Jew."

***

The long-awaited rematch with the Carolina Panthers pitted two teams on recent winning streaks, both making final, desperate pushes toward the playoffs. But for the day's loser, the season would, effectively, be over.

Perhaps it was the pressure of the situation that caused both teams to play so poorly. Or it

could have been the torrential rainstorms moving
through Charlotte that afternoon. Whatever the
reason, neither club made a convincing case for
itself as a playoff contender.

In fact the only aspect of the game distin-
guishing the two competitors occurred at the
hands of the referees. A dozen ill-timed penalties
against the Panthers turned an otherwise statisti-
cal dead-heat into a 20-7 Saints win.

It's hard to say which infraction proved most
costly: the Panther touchdown called back
because of holding; the phantom pass interfer-
ence call that gave the Saints a first-and-goal
from the Panther 1-yard-line; or the roughing-
the-kicker penalty that occurred on a 62-yard
field-goal attempt, giving the Saints new life and
ultimately leading to a touchdown.

Illegal procedure, too many men on the field,
offsides, encroachment, clipping, unsportsman-
like conduct, you name it, the zebras called
it...against Carolina. Not even the coach's instant
replay challenges went the Panthers' way.

A cynical man might have thought someone
had paid off the refs. But to the Fontana family,
watching on television back in Arabi, and to
Charmaine, dancing on the sidelines in her rain
slicker, it was all to obvious that the Pope's
dispensation was already paying dividends,
regardless of Oleg's faith.

Week 17
7 Wins, 8 Losses

Ron Beauchamp walked into the negotiations
at the State Capitol in Baton Rouge looking more
like a down-on-his-luck hobo than a high-
powered businessman. His face was unshaven,
his hair was disheveled, his suit looked like he'd
slept in it, and his eyes were glazed in the same
manner as victims of natural disasters...or
veterans of combat.

In a sense, Ron Beauchamp was in combat.
Because he was fighting tooth and nail to hold on
to everything he had worked to attain in his 77
years of living. Watching it all fall apart in such
a short time had nearly sent him over the edge.

"Where have you been?" Byron Fielding said,
as Beauchamp took a seat at a long conference
table. "I've been trying to get ahold of you for
the last 24 hours. We haven't gone over our
gameplan. We haven't coordinated our stories.
We're a shambles."

"You got a lot of room to talk," Beauchamp

said, noticing the bags under Fielding's eyes and the battered ball-point pen he'd chewed like a dog toy. "You look like hell."

Fielding shook his head. "I just haven't been myself since Minka left."

"Adamowicz?"

Fielding nodded.

"That woman really ate your lunch."

"I can't explain it. I haven't been able to eat. I can't sleep. I can't think straight. I don't know what to do."

"That's love for ya," Beauchamp said.

"Well, don't worry about me," Fielding said. "If there's one thing that calms my mind, it's analyzing spreadsheets. But you, Ron, this could be the most important meeting of your life, and you, you...is that alcohol I smell? It's not even ten o'clock."

Beauchamp patted Fielding on the shoulder and closed the binder sitting on the table in front of them. "Forget about all that," Beauchamp said, a peaceful look in his eyes. "I've got it all figured out."

"What do you mean?"

Beauchamp jutted his chin towards the door as Governor Fontenot entered the room, accompanied by Jim Burton, Chairman of the Louisiana Superdome Commission.

"Gentlemen," Governor Fontenot said, greeting her adversaries with a handshake.

"Governor," Beauchamp said.

Taking her seat at the table beside Burton, the governor adopted the practiced, comforting tone of an experienced politician and said, "Ron, before we get started, I want to offer my heartfelt condolences for your loss at Beau Maison."

Of course, considering that any setbacks to the Mississippi gaming industry would liklely bring additional revenues to Louisiana's own casinos, Beauchamp found the sincerity in the remark glaringly absent. But he did his best to maintain a civil tone.

"I'm beginning to wonder if God is a woman," he said with a chuckle. "Maybe my four ex-wives have gotten together and started a prayer circle."

Fielding fulfilled his obligation to supply a hearty laugh, but Fontenot found no humor in the comment. She lowered her eyes and began flipping through a binder of her own.

As Fielding prepared to initiate the negotiations, Beauchamp cut him off and leaned forward in his chair.

"Governor, before we get too far into this, I want to say up front that we have a new proposal that we'd like to put on the table.

Fontenot looked up from her notes. "Oh really, what's that?" she said, almost as if to dare Beauchamp. Meanwhile, Fielding turned to his boss, perplexed. They had not discussed any new proposal. Far as he understood, they were prepared to play hardball until the final out.

"We are prepared to forgo construction of All Saints Stadium in exchange for renovation of the Superdome and a one-time cash payment of..."

Beauchamp's voice dropped off and his words slurred together unrecognizably.

"What was that?" Fontenot said.

"One hundred million dollars," Beauchamp said. "In cash."

Fontenot erupted in a taunting laugh.

"You can't be serious, Ron," Jim Burton said.

The governor lowered her voice as if the deal on the table were somehow illegal. "Do I understand correctly that you are trying to extort money from the State of Louisiana to keep the Saints in New Orleans?"

Beauchamp pursed his lips but remained resolute. "Call it what you want, Governor, but it's what the Saints organization needs if it's to remain a financially viable operation."

"And just where do you propose we get a hundred million dollars?" Burton said. "That kind of money's not just laying around in some slush fund somewhere."

Beauchamp grinned and sneered. "Aw come on, don't try to fool me. This is Louisiana."

"Not any more it's not, " Fontenot said, slamming her binder shut.

Fielding tugged at Beauchamp's sleeve.

"Ron, this isn't what we talked about."

Ignoring the protest, Beauchamp pressed on. "How you get the money isn't really my concern, Governor, as long as you get it."

Fontenot cast her eyes toward the ceiling and scratched her chin. "Well, let's see. Should we take it from the public school textbook fund? Or how about we kick a few thousand poor children off the subsidized healthcare program? Do either of those options sound good to you?"

"You don't have to get ugly about it," Beauchamp said. "This is business. It isn't personal."

"Ha. You wanna' bet it's personal?" she said. "When you take away people's opportunity for a decent education, when you take away people's right to basic healthcare, just so a few fat, rich, white men can get fatter and richer, it's personal alright. Very personal."

"Who is she calling fat?" Fielding said.

"If it's not personal, how do you explain this?" Burton said, sliding an opened manila folder across the table. "The $700,000 yacht you bought last May for your wife, using Saints' funds – or should I say state funds?"

Beauchamp stared at the document, startled.

"That was a legitimate business expense," Fielding said, coming to the rescue, "based on the amount of entertaining necessary to conduct business at a level commensurate with ownership of an NFL franchise. There was nothing inappropriate about that deal."

Fontenot rolled her eyes.

"Maybe so," Burton said, "but what about this one?" He slid another folder across the table. "Funneling $30 million from the Saints to BMI might raise a lot of eyebrows."

"Let me see that," Beauchamp said, reaching for the folder. I don't know where you got this."

"Seems some of your very own people don't like the tricks you're trying to pull," Fontenot said. "You got a snitch inside your operation."

"Oh, I almost forgot," Burton said, sliding a third folder over. "The million-dollar hunting lodge in Arkansas. Again, bought with money from the taxpayers of Louisiana."

Fielding tried to act indignant. "This is all ludicrous. Tell her, Ron."

Beauchamp closed the folder and rocked back in his chair, clasping his fingers behind his head and smiling. "That's impressive. Actually, it's quite impressive. But don't forget about my condo in Destin and my $3 million RV. Since we're uncovering all the dirt."

"Ron, what the hell are you doing?" Fielding said. "You're out of your mind."

"No, Byron, I'm seeing things all too clearly," Beauchamp said.

"You do realize your proposed stadium deal is as dead as your sex life without Viagra," Fontenot said. "And you may as well forget about that hundred million while you're at it."

"Oh yes, I realize that," Beauchamp said, a contented tone in his voice. His lips curled into a smile at having secured the one thing he wanted when he walked in: an absolute deal-breaker. Though it galled him to do so, selling the team was his only hope for salvation in the wake of the hurricane. With Fontenot killing his proposal, Beauchamp would now cry to the local press that he had no other choice.

"So, shall we just sign a new lease now and get this over with once and for all?" Fontenot said. She pushed a contract across the table.

Beauchamp pushed it back. "No, Governor, since you're forcing me into this position, I'm afraid I'm going to have to take the Saints onto the open market and sell."

"You can't be serious," Fontenot said.

"Serious as a heart attack."

Fontenot didn't bat an eye. "Funny. I talked with the league commissioner just last week, and he tells me he really wants to keep a franchise in New Orleans. In fact, it's one of his favorite host cities for the Super Bowl. I think you'd have a hard time getting approval to sell to anyone who wanted to take the team to another market."

"Los Angeles is the number two media market in the U.S.," Beauchamp fired back. "And the average high temperature in early February is 75 degrees. Perfect for a Super

Bowl. I think they could get over the team leaving New Orleans."

Undaunted, Fontenot adopted a wry smile, indicating she was clearly enjoying the exchange. "That may be true, but if anything should happen to the Saints, I hear there's a madam down in the Quarter who might just have something to say about a few NFL executives, not to mention a few of the owners. It could get ugly.

"And besides, the commissioner tells me the L.A. consortium has already tendered an offer for the Minnesota Vikings. Like my NaNa used to say, 'You're a day late and a dollar short.'"

The look on Beauchamp's face told the governor that she had gotten the better of her adversary, but she couldn't leave it at that. Drunk on power and bloodlust, she sought to plunge the sword in deeper.

"You know, now that I think about it," she said, turning to Jim Burton, "if he's already asking us to put up a hundred mil, why don't we just go whole-hog and buy the team outright?"

"Ha," Beauchamp said, "you said yourself the state could never afford it."

"Well, who knows, maybe we *do* have some kind of slush fund somewhere. After all, this *is* Louisiana, isn't it?"

Now it was Jim Burton's turn to try and rein in his boss. "Governor, what are you doing? We can't buy a football team..." Underneath the table, Fontenot ground the pointed heel of her business pump into the top of Burton's foot.

"Be careful, Jenny. Six hundred million dollars is a lot of money," Beauchamp said.

"No really," Burton said. "We can't..."

"Three hundred," Fontenot said.

"Is this a negotiation?" Beauchamp said.

"Okay," Fontenot said. "Three-fifty."

"Governor, this is beyond the scope of today's discussion," Fielding said.

Beauchamp actually felt relieved that Fielding had jumped in. Given his desperate state, who knows what kind of deal he'd be willing to make?

"Fielding's right, Governor. You wouldn't want to start something you can't finish."

"No, Ron, that's your territory, the way you men always leave us women hanging."

"That's it," Beauchamp said, throwing up his hands in disgust. "I didn't come here to get insulted. Consider this negotiation finished." He pushed back his chair and signaled for Fielding to join in his abrupt departure. Despite the frown on his face, inside he was almost smiling.

***

www.saintsforum.com
Posted by baghead 12:19 CT
Check this out...
If the Saints move to Los Angeles, New Orleans will be responsible for the two screwiest sports names ever: the Utah Jazz and the Los Angeles Saints!!

Posted by C-money 12:22 CT
Re: Check this out...
Se habla espanol? It makes perfect sense for the
City of Angels to have a team nicknamed the Saints.

Posted by Landlord 12:44 CT
All talk, no action
Beauchamp is just blowing smoke. I told these bozos
the other day that the Saints aren't going anywhere.

Posted by RemyMartin 1:03 CT
Fontenot hates football
As long as Guv Fontenot is in office, it doesn't look
good for us Saints fans. I am a die-hard fan, win or
lose, and the last thing I want to see is the Saints
move, but it wouldn't bother Fontenot a bit if they left.
She's just a typical woman who doesn't like football.

Posted by Katt 1:09 CT
Being a woman...
Has nothing to do with it. I'm a woman, and I love
football. Fontenot is just sick and tired of giving free-
loaders like Beauchamp millions in tax money while
the schools have gone to pot and the poverty rate
has gone through the roof. 80% of the voters in
Louisiana agree with her. What would you do in her
shoes? Let's face it. New Orleans is too small and
too poor for an NFL team. It has much bigger
problems. Use the tax dollars for schools and roads,
not extortion to pro team owners.

Posted by Kingfish 1:12 CT
Re: Being a woman...
Fontenot is an idiot. She's running this state into the
ground. She won't acknowledge the team's economic
impact on the city and state, even though it was well
documented by an economist at UNO.

Posted by fa-real 1:15 CT
Re: Being a woman...
Aw come on, Kingfish. That guy was a shill for the
Saints. You can't use those numbers. Who do you
think funded that study in the first place?

Posted by Humerus 1:24 CT
Re: Being a woman...
So let's see, we let the Saints go and all will be well
with the schools and poverty, right? Oh, and then a
bunch of Fortune 500 companies will want to come
and set up shop in New Orleans.

Posted by Uptown Brown 1:30 CT
Greed
Beauchamp's only concern is making money. There's
nothing wrong with money, but how much is enough?
If you knew that he was making a 30% profit each
year on the football operations, would you still want
to subsidize him with taxpayer money just because
other NFL owners are making 100% profit?

Posted by Batman 1:42 CT
Re: Check this out...
My brother works for Beau Maison, and he says
Beauchamp is putting the entire operation up for
sale, including the Saints, because he's flat broke.

Posted by Hoops 1:50 CT
Fontenot's got Beauchamp
Beauchamp can't go anywhere and Fontenot knows
this. She isn't going to give in to anything and
Beauchamp is going to have to stay put.

Posted by FrankG 1:52 CT
Re: Fontenot's got Beauchamp
She needs to tell that greedy old bastard to shove it.

Posted by Manayak 1:55 CT
Re: Fontenot's got Beauchamp
The Saints are gone after next year, when they have
an out on their contract. The team is in a small, dying
market and cannot survive without taxpayer subsi-
dies. Remember, Fontenot got elected by saying she
would cut off welfare to pro sports teams. If 80% of
the people in the state agree with her, it would be
political suicide if Fontenot gives Beauchamp what
he wants. So kiss the Saints goodbye.

Posted by Lutcher 1:59 CT
Only one problem
Now what the hell are we gonna' do on Sundays?

                            ***

    Tired of waiting for Oleg to take the initiative
in their budding relationship, Charmaine heeded
her mother's advice and tried to make inroads to
his heart through his stomach. Showing up at
practice with a couple of po-boys as the team
was finishing, she invited Oleg to join her for a
picnic on the levee just down the road.

    Oleg made quick work of his oyster, dressed,
his new favorite meal, and he sat quietly watching a gulf-bound tanker plowing down the
Mississippi, while the late afternoon sun began to
set. Poor Charmaine was pushing the boundaries
of her mental capacity searching for things in
common with Oleg, although something told her
there was a legitimate connection.

    Well, for starters, she thought he was smokin'
hot...and mysterious...and gifted. And he seemed

reasonably interested in her. But aside from that, about the only thing they'd really shared was the secret of Oleg's Jewish faith, which had now been exposed to everyone like a flasher at Mardi Gras. Surely, there had to be a way to get this guy to open up.

Finally, after a little too much silence, Charmaine blurted out, "Look, if you wanna' convert, I'm sure Father Joe would be more than happy to put you on the Express Plan."

Oleg took several moments to collect his thoughts before responding. "Thank you for the offer, Charmaine, but I am not sure I want to be part of any religion."

"Then why do you keep tellin' people you're a Jew?" Charmaine said, crinkling her brow. "It's like every chance you get, 'I am Jew. I am Jew.' You're like a proud queer keeps comin' outta' da closet to everybody he knows."

"Because it is who I am."

"But I thought you just said..."

"It is complicated, I know."

Charmaine polished off the last of her roast beef and swiss, dressed, and started licking gravy off her fingers, one by one. "It ain't complicated at all," she said almost absent-mindedly, implying it was the simplest thing in the world, which it was for someone who didn't do nuance. "Just follow what you believe."

"But that is the problem. I do not believe

what I am supposed to."

"Then what do you believe? Do you even
believe in God?"

Oleg blinked hard in an attempt to reappraise
the woman sitting across from him. For a split-
second, he felt a twinge of anger. Who was she to
question his beliefs? But after the irritation
subsided, he felt something altogether different,
an abiding respect, a desire to know her. Though
he'd never admit it, in that moment, Oleg began
to see Charmaine as an actual human being.

"Of course I believe in God," he said. "Is
other parts I do not know. All these books. They
are written by man. Why is one man right and
other wrong? Who is to say? Especially when
words of one man cause pain to another. That is
not word of God. Word of God lives in heart. Is
same for all people."

"But people need something to believe in,"
Charmaine said, "somebody to lead the way."

"Is just like people coming to me, thinking I
am messiah. I am just a man. I am no different."

"But you are different," Charmaine said.

"Well, maybe a little," Oleg said, "but I am
no better. Nobody is. Christian. Jew. Muslim. If
one is right, then does everyone else burn in hell?
That is ridiculous. Means majority of world is
doomed to hell. Ridiculous. That is not word of
God. Word of God is love, peace. Everything else
is tool to open heart and mind. If religion closes

mind, is work of Devil, not God."

Charmaine looked alarmed. "So you sayin' religion is the work of the devil?"

"No, no, please. Do not misunderstand. I am just saying...faith should bring man together, not tear people apart."

After gazing at the clouds in the sky for a moment, Charmaine perked up. "Hey, I got an idea," she said, framing the thought with her hands. "Why don't you stawt a new religion?"

Oleg shook off the suggestion like a winter chill. "World does not need new religion. We just need ones we have to get along. Is why sport is good, because it brings people together."

"Unless you're on the other team."

"But is only a game. People are not killing in name of Saint or Falcon."

"You obviously ain't never been to da French Quarta' after da Saints lose."

"You must know what I mean," Oleg said.

"I guess so. Maybe dat's why I ain't got a problem wit' bein' Catlick. Come to think of it, I remember when da Pope was here sayin' mass in da Dome, he even said, wait, let me get this right, he said religion ain't never a reason for fightin'."

"Really? Your Pope, Pope Pius, said this?"

"Well, lemme' think," Charmaine said, squinting to picture the scene in her mind. "No, wait, he said 'conflict.' Yeah, dat was da word he used. Religion ain't never a reason for conflict.

"I'm not makin' it up," she continued. "I can remember it plain as day, 'cause dat was right before he blessed a Zapp's potato chip dat looked like da Virgin Mary."

Oleg smiled. "I must read work of this Pope Pius. It sounds very encouraging."

"And who knows, maybe after that you'll want to convert."

"But I told you, I am..."

"I know, I know, a Jew, I got it. Well, look, here's an idea. If you're a Jew, stop runnin' from it and do what ya can to help open up people's minds and bring people together like ya said."

This ignited a spark in Oleg's memory. "Yes, I see. Is like my nigga' Double-D said to me when I first join Saint."

Charmaine grew stern. "Oleg, you really need to stop usin' dat N-word before somebody beats ya ass. It ain't polite."

"I am sorry, Charmaine," he said. "I mean no disrespect. I mean only to say I admire Dexter because he is proud of who he is. He does not run from it. I hope to be that way, too."

Charmaine relaxed and smiled again. "Well, yeah, you should. They got a lotta' messed up people in dis world dat ya can help. Who knows, maybe ya father will even come around."

"Oh, I do not know about that." Oleg clutched at a handful of grass and cocked his head to look at her. "You think it can work?"

From the gleam in his eyes, Charmaine could see she had finally connected with him, and it made her heart swell.

"Sure it can," she said. "You're famous. And people listen to you because ya don't try to pull no B.S. Besides, it's better than shuttin' ya'self off from everybody. Far as I'm concerned, I don't care what ya are, so long as you're honest wit' ya'self and you're happy. Life's too short to be miserable all the time."

"So, all this time, you think I am miserable?" Oleg said, troubled by the observation.

"Oh no, don't get me wrong. I think you're... amazing. And I want ya to stay dat way."

Oleg's face lit up. "Well, I am never miserable when I am with you."

"Aw stop, you're makin' me blush."

"Is true, Charmaine. You have removed cloud from my brain. For such a beautiful woman, you are very wise."

"Well, since I helped you out, can ya do somethin' for me?"

"Anything."

"You been layin' ya hands on everybody and their cousin 'round here. How 'bout layin' ya hands on me?"

Oleg fidgeted. "I am not sure I understand."

Pouncing on him like a hungry lioness, Charmaine wrapped her arms around Oleg and pulled him in for a kiss.

***

At 7-8 and riding the crest of a team-record seven-game win streak, the Saints had set up their fans for perhaps their most spectacular letdown yet. But in spite of the countless disappointments and heartbreaks, a capacity crowd filled the Dome for the final regular season game against the Green Bay Packers.

At 11-4, the Pack had already wrapped up the NFC Central Division title, and all signs indicated they would be resting star quarterback Brad Oubre and practically the entire starting lineup. Prior to the game, the Saints presented Oubre – a native of nearby Picayune, Mississippi – with an official No. 5 team jersey. Despite Oubre's never having actually played for the Saints, area fans regarded him as one of their own, cheering him over the course of his 12-year career, during which he earned an MVP honor, four divisional championships, two NFC titles and one Super Bowl victory, which took place in the Dome six years earlier.

The Saints would need a complex series of events to occur in order to make the playoffs as a wildcard. But for these fans, starved as they'd been of tangible success for so long, this game took on the specter of an actual playoff game. Considering the Saints had to win to have any shot whatsoever, it *was* a playoff game, and the atmosphere was reflected in the decibel level, not to mention the array of creative costumes. Of particular note were the scores of fans sporting black vinyl bodybags, the newest addition to the collection of great fan get-ups that included the Cheesehead, Darth Raider, and the Hogs.

Playing only one series, Oubre marched the team downfield in seven plays, capping off the opening drive with an 11-yard touchdown strike to put the Packers ahead 7-0.

The Saints responded with a quick strike of their own, as Robbie Gauthier hit Dexter Douglass on a 38-yard fly pattern to even the score. After a Saint pickoff of Packer backup Carl Mortensen, Cedric Wilson bulled his way to 43 yards on four carries, going in untouched on the final seven and giving the Saints a 14-7 lead.

Two defensive stops and two Oleg Adamowicz field goals, from 37 and 32 yards, gave the Saints a 20-7 halftime lead. And after a dominating 8-minute touchdown drive to open the second half and go up 27-7, it looked like the Saints were on their way to 8-8.

But that's when Mortensen found his range, and the dormant Packer running attack found its legs. In the blink of an eye, Green Bay had scored twice to pull within 27-21. Meanwhile, Jake Radke and his staff had reverted to their early-season pattern of conservative playcalling, resulting in successive three-and-outs.

The somber mood in the dome was palpable,

and it wasn't due to the dozen or so fans wearing bodybags who had to be carried from the stands on stretchers, having passed out from excessive alcohol consumption coupled with a lack of ventilation inside the costumes. Rather, it was caused by the painful memories and the foreboding sense of déjà vu: the disastrous Monday Night Meltdown against the Raiders in 1979; the Prevent-Defense Putdown against the Rams in 1983; the Coulda', Woulda' Shoulda' fiasco against the 49ers in 1987.

When the alarm clock sounded with 1:52 remaining in the fourth quarter, the Saints found themselves trailing 28-27, looking to add yet another chapter in their tragic saga.

What happened next would be forever etched in the minds of all those who witnessed it and even some who didn't, subject to retelling among friends, co-workers, and grandkids for generations to come.

Jordash Jones botched the ensuing kickoff, giving the Saints the ball at their own 7-yard-line with 1:40 to play and no timeouts. On the first play from scrimmage, Radke inexplicably called a draw for Cedric, fooling no one and promptly losing two yards. As valuable time ticked off the clock, fans wasted no time showing their displeasure with the call, issuing a barrage of boos.

With 1:20 to play, Gauthier hit Dexter on a deep out for 16 yards, but he was unable to get out of bounds to stop the clock. The new set of downs, however, enabled Gauthier to spike the ball with :53 to play. Given the way Oleg had been kicking lately, the Saints only needed about 40 yards to get within his range. Still plenty of time for that.

On second-and-ten from the 21, after finding no one open downfield, Gauthier dumped the ball off to Cedric out of the backfield, and he scampered to the sideline for 8 yards. A quick out to Dexter yielded 5 yards and another first down with 36 ticks on the clock. Gauthier then misfired on two consecutive long pass plays, leaving 18 seconds. On third down, he hit Jordash for 8 yards and a first down. But even though the clock stopped, a mere six seconds remained.

Faced with perhaps the biggest decision of his career – try for a 58-yard Hail Mary or a 75-yard field goal, Jake Radke didn't hesitate one second.

"'Leg," he said, "why don't you go on and try that drop-kick thing you did a couple of weeks back. What the hell."

Without batting an eye, Oleg donned his helmet and trotted onto the field to deafening cheers and rhythmic chants of "O-Leg, O-Leg, O-Leg."

The Packers burned their final timeout trying to ice the stoic kicker. The big-screen closeup of Oubre on the sidelines showed him to be smiling and jawing with teammates and, generally, loving the drama of the moment, unconcerned about the ultimate outcome. A subsequent closeup of Oleg revealed a look of concern comparable to when he does his laundry.

In the broadcast booth, Tim Anderson and CoCo Pichon braced themselves for the call, trying to summon the words that would salve the wounds of listeners should the kick fall short. Inside Oleg's head, all was quiet as he engaged in his standard pre-kick ritual, a wordless combination of visualization, Zen meditation, and something resembling prayer.

At the moment the ball was snapped, there was an instant of silence, as though every one of the 75,000 gathered had sucked in a breath simultaneously. The candle-power of the thousands of camera flashes popping at the same time inside the Dome could have lit the stadium should power have gone out at that moment.

But once the ball sailed squarely through the uprights, giving the Saints a 30-28 victory as time expired, the pent-up energy in the building erupted like a volcano, and fans celebrated what might potentially go down as the biggest win in team history. All that remained was the wait for a trio of other games to conclude to determine whether the Saints had earned a wildcard berth or an unwanted vacation.

Wildcard Round
8 Wins, 8 Losses

After the Chicago Bears, Seattle Seahawks, and Washington Redskins all botched their playoff chances in rapid succession, the Saints found themselves squarely in the postseason for the first time in team history, and they laid claim to several other distinctions in the process: they were the first 8-8 team to ever reach the playoffs; their eight-game winning streak was the longest in team history; and their enigmatic kicker, Oleg Adamowicz, had rewritten virtually every kicking record in the book.

Oleg had learned to tolerate the press in recent weeks, but the ensuing media onslaught following his heroic kick was more than he could stomach. Previously, coaches and teammates had granted him the space he desired, not wanting to upset their prized player's delicate mental state. But the national media were a different story. At first, it was the phone that would not stop ringing. But Oleg solved that problem by unplugging it. He didn't own an answering machine, so it wasn't necessary to check his messages.

That's when Saints director of public relations Jackie Potter intervened, cornering Oleg at team practice. Not wanting to let this rare PR opportunity go to waste, Jackie not only acquiesced to each and every interview request, she also agreed to allow camera crews from ESPN, Fox, and NFL Films to tail the kicker throughout the week for special feature segments. A fourth crew was even on hand to package a segment for the burgeoning NFL Europe market. Rather than dampening their interest, Oleg's ambivalence to fame and his disregard for the trappings of Western success only served to make him a more intriguing subject.

The cameras were even on hand when Oleg retrieved an unusual letter from his mailbox. With Fox correspondent Katie Carlson present at his side to document the poignance of the scene, an otherwise typical under-the-helmet feature took on the schmaltzy melodrama of reality TV at its best.

"What is it?" Carlson said, softening her voice in that tone newscasters adopt to show concern. "Can you tell us?"

Oleg walked into the house studying the jagged handwriting on the pages. He seemed transported to another realm, blind to the presence of anyone else. The letter itself bore the multi-colored markings of air mail, and the battered envelope looked as though it had, in fact, endured a transcontinental voyage.

Eyes still fixated on the letter, Oleg replied in a defeated tone. "Is from father in Poland."

"He must be very proud of you," Carlson said, smiling. But when Oleg looked up from the letter, she could see that his eyes had grown red and puffy, telling a different story.

"No," Oleg said. "We do not often speak. He does not approve of sport."

Carlson moved closer and motioned for the two of them to have a seat on the...floor. "But doesn't he see the joy you bring to so many people with your talent?"

Sitting cross-legged beside her, Oleg tossed the pages on the floor between them while a cameraman hovered behind Carlson's shoulder.

"He only sees what he wants to see. That sport is meaningless. Cheap thrill. That I have turned my back on my family. I do not expect you to understand. Myself, I do not understand. Is why we do not speak."

For dramatic effect, Carlson reached out and scooped up the letter. She tried to make out the text on the page but could see it was not written in English. "Well if you don't speak, what's the letter about? It must be something special."

Oleg turned toward the cameraman, searching in vain for someone to give him a reprieve from

the inquisition. He tried to answer but had to
fight to keep his emotions under control.

"With money from new contract next year, I
wanted to build him house in Poland," Oleg said.
"Get him out of ghetto."

"Oh, that is so touching," Carlson said,
reaching out to pat him on the knee.

"But he does not want it. He says I have
shamed him."

Carlson knew she had an Emmy-award-
winning moment here, and she was determined to
milk the interview for all it was worth.

"How can that be?" she said. "Doesn't he
know you're the Pope's favorite football player?"

Oleg laughed. "That only makes it worse. For
Jews like my father, even acknowledging Yeshua
is strictly forbidden."

Carlson gasped. "I had no idea. Are there
really people who still think like that?"

"Yes, for some there is much tension between
faiths," Oleg said.

"How does that make you feel?"

Oleg's shoulders sagged. "Sad. Very sad."

Carlson signaled to her cameraman to zoom
in for a closeup, hoping to catch a tear rolling
down Oleg's cheek. But none was forthcoming.

"If you could look into the camera and talk to
your father right now, is there something you'd
like to tell him?"

Oleg shook his head. "It does not matter. He

does not watch television."

"Well, just imagine for a second, if you could talk to him, what would you say?"

Oleg sucked in a deep breath and thought it over for a second before looking into the camera. "I would tell him that I have accepted who I am. That I believe in Torah. Maybe not in the same way as him. But I once heard a wise man say, 'We all walk a different path but reach the same destination.'"

"Really. Who was that?"

"Pope Pius."

"Wise man, indeed," Carlson said in her typical vapid style. "Do you love him?"

"The Pope?"

"No, your father?"

"Of course I love him," Oleg said. "All my life, I have only tried to honor him, to make him proud of me, but somehow I have failed."

"Oleg, nobody thinks you're a failure," Carlson said.

"It does not matter," Oleg said, waving her off. "At day's end, I must be true to myself, to what is in my heart – this is God, is where the spirit lives, where I find peace."

When Oleg looked back at Carlson, she had produced a kleenex and was dabbing at the corners of her eyes. "That's so beautiful. Can I give you a hug?"

Before he could respond, she had seized upon

him like a starlet on a middle-aged movie pro-
ducer, and the camera kept rolling to capture the
segment that would set female football fans to
swooning over the latest NFL heartthrob.

***

Beauchamp and Fielding sat alone in the
empty coaches' conference room inside the
Saints' training facility, going over the final
details of their presentation to the media gathered
in the adjacent press room. While flipping through
his collected papers, Fielding found a phone
message slip and held it up for Beauchamp to see.

"Did you ever return the Archbishop's call?"
Fielding said. "He's called three times now."

"Yeah, right," Beauchamp said. "He either
wants to bug me about my pledge to the church
fund or guilt me about our Dome negotiations,
neither one good. I got more important things to
deal with right now in case you haven't noticed."

"Just trying to be polite."

"We can't afford to be polite any more."

With the Saints' first-ever playoff game only
days away, the hastily called press conference
couldn't have come at a worse time from a
coaches', players', or fans' perspective. But from
a purely business standpoint, the timing was
brilliant, given the "buy low / sell high" gospel of
any good dealmaker. A week ago, the Saints
would have been just another losing franchise
looking to make a fresh start. Today, they were

the hottest, up-and-coming team in the league, sure to command top dollar on the open market, wherever they might land.

"I still can't get over that stunt you pulled with Fontenot," Fielding said, recalling the last unsuccessful negotiation with the governor. "The way you forced her hand like that, it was a stroke of genius."

Beauchamp, however, looked like he had a bad case of heartburn and didn't want to hear it. "Nothing brilliant about it. Desperation'll make a genius out of the least of us." He rubbed his forehead and stared at the table. "I still can't believe it's come to this."

Fielding slapped him on the shoulder and smiled, trying to buck up his spirits. "Look at it this way, Ron. You're gonna' come out of this thing smelling like a rose. You're gonna' clear six hundred million easy on the deal. You'll be able to salvage the entire Beau Maison operation. Probably, you'll even have enough left over to invest in bringing another team back here after the Saints leave. This isn't just a win-win situation. It's a win-win-win."

Beauchamp turned and glared at his most trusted financial advisor like he was the towel boy. "How many times do I have to tell you, Byron, I never wanted to sell? I don't want the team to leave. I just want...aw what the hell. You're not from here. You'll never understand."

"Now, Ron, there is no need to get overdramatic about this. "

"Forget about it. It's too late to turn back now," Beauchamp said, pushing himself to his feet. "Let's go get this thing over with."

Without awaiting a response, he walked out to face the gathered media, announcing his intention to sell the New Orleans Saints football club to the highest bidder.

***

The moment Governor Fontenot heard the breaking news of the Saints' impending sale, she and her entire staff went into crisis mode.

Despite possessing reams of information on Beauchamp's malfeasance in handling Saints' business affairs – the $30 million funnelled to BMI, the RV, the boat, the condo – she had yet to go public with any of it, hoping, rather, to use it as leverage in the ongoing negotiations. Now, Beauchamp had beaten her to the punch. Releasing the evidence at this point might temporarily shift the blame off of her, but it wouldn't solve the problem.

If she didn't act quickly and decisively, this situation could not only become a public relations disaster for her administration, it would spell doom for any potential re-election campaign, despite what current poll numbers said.

To be sure, she was in a no-win position: if she caved in to Beauchamp's terms, she would be perceived as soft, thus reinforcing the stereotype of women as weak that had plagued them for centuries, and she would draw fire from her liberal base for shelling out more corporate welfare to the already wealthy owner.

On the contrary, if she didn't broker a deal, as was shaping up, she would open a Pandora's Box of accusations leveled in her direction: some would perceive her as overly emotional, thus reinforcing another stereotype plaguing women in professional settings; others would blame her simply because she let the Saints get away on her watch; regardless of the team's disputed economic impact, there was no denying the NFL franchise carried a unique cachet that couldn't be matched, no matter how many Arena Football or minor league hockey clubs were brought in to fill the void. Sundays just wouldn't be the same.

Having assembled the best minds in the state and summoned its top corporate leaders, Fontenot hunkered down for a marathon strategy session inside the Capitol on, of all days, New Year's Eve. But after 17 hours, including a break to watch Dick Clark's Rockin' Eve, the braintrust had reached a stalemate. The governor dismissed all her guests but Jim Burton, head of the Superdome Commission, and the two repaired to Fontenot's office in order to go over their meager options.

"Certainly, there must be something we're

overlooking," Fontenot said, stepping to the bar to prepare a neat scotch. "Are you sure we've explored every option?"

Burton rubbed his bleary eyes and flipped through the notepad resting in his lap. "You were there in the room, Jeanette. You saw what we have to work with."

"Let's just go through the list one more time," she said in between sips. "There's bound to be something we're missing. What was the problem with that rapper guy again?"

"Mister Q?" Burton said, reading from his notes. "Well, he is worth two hundred million and would be a great candidate for minority ownership, but he has that felony gun charge and is still on probation. The NFL Ownership Committee would never approve it."

"Damn," Fontenot said. "Isn't there something we can do, like a gubernatorial pardon?"

"Unfortunately, not in this case," Burton said.

Fontenot took another swig. "And Cal Perkins? I sure do love his fried chicken."

Burton refocused his eyes on the notepad and read aloud. "Let's see. His business has gone belly up since taking over rival Bishop's Fried Chicken. Lawsuit, bankruptcy, creditors, assets tied up. No good. Plus, he'd be competing with Double-D's. Wouldn't be good for team morale. "

Fontenot's pace picked up, and it was clear she was growing impatient. "How about that young kid in the room? Landry. The family owns a barge company. That's clean, right?"

"Jeanette, come on. You of all people should know. He was only there as a proxy for his old man, who's in prison with Edwin Edwards."

"Oh yeah. Damn!" she said. She tapped her index finger against her temple. "And Freeload McNoMad?"

"Well then you'd have the protestors..."

"But oil and gas exploration is legal."

"You're forgetting about their mining operations," Burton said. "Freeload mines in Sarawank and Bang Tango are the biggest producers of gold and copper in the world. Those countries also happen to be ruled by violent despots, which explains the U.N. sanctions against the company for doing business with rogue states. Besides, if Freeload buys the team, you'll have to do business with Billy Bob Madden."

"Freeload's CEO?"

"He put the 'Mad' in McNoMad."

"You do have a point," Fontenot said. "What else do we have?"

"Eternal Rest Enterprises."

"The cemetery company?"

"Full spectrum funeral services," Burton said. "Second biggest operator in America."

"They own graveyards. Not the kind of image New Orleans or Louisiana needs. What else? Why don't we look at state funding?"

"Governor, you heard it from your very own Treasurer. Louisiana doesn't have the money."

"Aw, but wouldn't it be something, Jim?" Fontenot said, running her finger around the rim of her glass. "That'd really show those pricks."

"I'm sorry. It's not gonna' happen."

"Yeah, you're right," she said grudgingly. "Well, maybe we could get the public to help. It's good enough for Green Bay. Why not us?"

"You'll never get it past the conservatives in the State Senate. They'll scream 'Socialism.'"

"But we won't be running it," she said.

"Somebody will have to."

"We can appoint some...oh, I see what you mean. But that's a good start. That's the kind of out-of-the-box thinking we're going to need to solve this problem."

"Well, Bill Gates' wife's father is from New Orleans. Maybe you can call Microsoft."

"Now that's what I'm talking about."

"And Richard Simmons is from New Orleans. He's made a mint off 'Sweatin' to the Oldies.'" Fontenot glared at Burton as though the suggestion were ludicrous.

"We could offer to make him an honorary Saintsation," he said. "Give him a pair of black and gold short-shorts."

"I like it," Fontenot said, checking her watch. "Give me more of that." She pulled her overcoat off the rack and grabbed her handbag.

"Where are you going?" Burton said.

"Church."

"Church? It's New Year's Day."

"Holy day of obligation. What can I say?"

"That reminds me," Burton said. "Did you ever return that call from Archbishop Boudreaux in New Orleans? Your secretary said he called four times and wanted to talk about the Saints."

"Oh right," Fontenot said, groaning. "He probably got word of our meeting, and with all the money-men in the room, wanted to get a seat at the table so he could hit 'em up for donations. But that would be completely inappropriate." Fontenot leaned close and lowered her voice, although the two were alone. "I hear the Church is really struggling."

"You sure that's what he wanted?" Burton said. "You didn't even call him back. Isn't that a sin or something?"

"Hey, I'm going to church, aren't I? I'll put an extra twenty in the collection basket. Meantime, you stay here and keep coming up with ideas. I'll be back in an hour."

"But we've already been here all night."

"The delirium will spur your creativity."

"But, but..."

"Oh alright, then take a nap or something. I'll be right back. But first I gotta' go pray. At this point, we need all the help we can get."

***

It would have been understandable if the Saints had laid an egg in their first-ever playoff game, but it was the Dallas Cowboys who looked like novices in their NFC Wildcard matchup at Texas Stadium.

An early interception of the Cowpokes' journeyman, 47-year-old quarterback, Vito Malefacto, helped the Saints race to an early 14-0 lead. And Cowboy coach Willie Starkist's old-school gameplan made Jake Radke's playcalling look innovative by comparison.

Considering the number of penalties, miscues, and poorly executed plays, the product on the field was virtually unwatchable. Nonetheless, Saints fans could revel in the team's 17-7 half-time lead and at least hope for more of the same.

A 37-yard touchdown run by Cowboy rookie Kendrell Davenport midway through the third quarter helped narrow the gap to 17-14. But the Saints responded with a long drive, on which Robbie Gauthier went 7-for-8 for 56 yards. Cedric Wilson capped it off with a 6-yard scamper around left end for the score.

On the next possession, Malefacto botched the snap from center, and the Saints recovered inside Cowboy territory. When the Saints' drive stalled, Oleg was able to connect on a 46-yard field goal, upping the lead again to 10 points.

As time wound down in the fourth quarter and the Cowboys' desperation grew, Malefacto got hot on a hurry-up drive that resulted in a 12-yard touchdown toss with just over three minutes to play. The Cowboys then forced the Saints into a three-and-out, finally igniting the crowd.

With 1:30 to go and Cowboy returner Troy Black set up to field the punt at his own 40-yard line, the stage was set for them to tie or even win the game in dramatic fashion.

But in a rare display of irony, the football gods smote the Cowboys in one fell swoop, as if to punish the team for their excesses throughout their heyday of the 1990s.

Losing sight of the ball as it traveled from the open air to the covered portion of the field, Black muffed the punt and watched helplessly as it bounced right into the arms of Saint special teams specialist Mike Jones, a fan favorite who had been working as a UPS driver less than one year earlier. Talk about a special delivery.

As disgruntled Cowboy fans jeered their team, the Saints were able to kill the final 1:18, walking away with the organization's first postseason victory and a chance to meet former NFC West rival the San Francisco 49ers in the next round.

Divisional Playoff Round
9 Wins, 8 Losses

While it was true that Oleg and Charmaine had yet to consummate their relationship, had yet to even go out on a formal date, nonetheless, she went ballistic when she watched that little strumpet Katie Carlson putting the moves on her guy on national television.

A.J. Fontana, being a man of traditional Italian mindset, did the only appropriate thing upon seeing his daughter's distress: he decided to pay Oleg a visit. He hadn't thought through his plan and wasn't exactly sure what he would say. But as the elder Fontana surveyed the neighborhood surrounding Oleg's South Miro Street duplex, he harkened back to his own boyhood home in the Lower Ninth Ward and felt a strange connection to the Polish-born kicker. Despite their outward differences, A.J. knew that he and Oleg were cut from similar cloth.

"Mister A.J.," Oleg said, surprised to receive a visitor before 9 a.m. "What brings you here? Is everything okay?"

A.J. pulled his hands out of his jacket pockets, where they'd been warming from the light winter chill. Given his Sicilian heritage, he was physically incapable of speaking while the movement of his hands was restricted.

"I'm sorry to botha' ya, Alex," A.J. said, "but I wanted to talk wit' ya as soon as possible." He cast a glance behind him to make sure no one was following. "Is it okay if I come in? If Charmaine knew I was here right now, she'd have a cow."

Oleg hesitated. "But, home is not clean..."

A.J. brushed this aside and pushed his way past. "Aw, don't worry about it. I was a bachelor once." Upon entering, however, he was startled to find such stark furnishings. The room looked much as it always did, mattress on the floor, small pile of dirty clothes in the corner next to the oversized duffel that served as Oleg's closet. A single book on the floor beside the bed. This time it was *Don Quixote*.

"Sure could use a woman's touch," A.J. said, laughing uneasily. He looked around for an appropriate place to sit, opting in the end to remain standing. "Alex, I know you and my Charmaine have gotten real close these last few months, and I wanted to come over and tell ya, Miss Shirley and I, well, we couldn't be happier. We think you are a fine, upstandin' young man, and our Charmaine is lucky to have you."

"Thank you, sir," Oleg said. "Is very kind."

"After seein' dat story on da television, what with ya father shuttin' ya out and all, I wanted to come over and tell ya...you're always welcome in our family...long as ya take good care of our Charmaine, of course."

Oleg froze momentarily as the statement sunk in, and he summoned the words to respond. "But you are Catholic and I am..."

"Forget about it," A.J. said. "Far as I'm concerned, dat's a non-issue. To be honest, it's my wife who's the devout one in our family. I'm only Catholic in da sense dat da church I *don't* go to on Sundays is a Catholic one. Last time I stepped foot was..." A.J. scratched his head while searching his memory. "My buddy Mickey Palermo's funeral. Anyway, what's important is dat you and Charmaine care for each other. You make each other happy. And let's face it, she ain't gettin' any younger."

A.J. jabbed Oleg in the side with an elbow and gave a playful chuckle.

"I, I do not know what to say. Thank you. That means a lot to me."

"And when da time is right," A.J. said, resuming his warm tone, "when you're ready to pop da question, I want ya to know dat you have Miss Shirley's and my full blessin'."

"Please, let me try to understand. You are

offering Charmaine's hand in marriage?"

"Well, basically."

"I thought I was to ask you for hand."

"Well, yeah, but I jus' figured I'd circumcise the process."

"So, does this mean you offer dowry, too?"

Dowry? A.J. wasn't sure what a dowry was, but it didn't sound like anything he'd be offering. "Son, I'll have you know that my Charmaine is a perfectly respectable young woman," he said, almost indignant. "I'll offer nothing of da kind."

"But we have yet to..."

A.J. threw an arm around Oleg's shoulder and lowered his voice like he was sharing a secret with a friend. "You don't need to pussyfoot around with me, 'Leg. I seen dese otha' bozos she brings around, da way dey fall hard and fast for her. But you're in a different league. And I'm not sayin' dat jus' because you're a football staw and all. We jus' wanna' be ready if things progress to da next level. Know what I mean?"

Outside, Oleg heard the sound of tires screeching and a car door slamming. In seconds, a visitor was banging on Oleg's door.

"Charmaine," Oleg said upon answering.

She burst through the door, walking past Oleg to confront her father.

"Daddy, what the hell are you doing here?"

"Sunshine, I was jus'..."

"Gawd, dis is so embarrassin'," Charmaine

said. "Daddy, I'm a grown woman, I don't need you buttin' into my love life."

She turned to Oleg. "I didn't have nothin' to do wit' dis. I swear to Gawd."

"But baby," A.J. said, "I was jus' tellin' Alex dat no matter what his father says, he's welcome in our family. Honest."

"Really? Is dat true?" she said.

Both A.J. and Oleg nodded. Charmaine calmed down enough to catch her breath.

"And he offer your hand in marriage," Oleg said, cutting through the brief silence.

"You *what*?" Charmaine shrieked at her father. "Jesus, Mary, and Joseph." She buried her face in her hands. "I never been so humiliated in all my life."

"But baby..." A.J. said.

Oleg stepped to Charmaine's side and attempted to pull her upright to gain her attention.

"Charmaine," Oleg said. "Is okay. Really."

Slowly, she rose up, revealing teary eyes and flushed cheeks.

"Really?" she said to Oleg, thinking for an instant that she may have finally hooked one. "You mean..."

Oleg proceeded cautiously, not wanting to commit himself to anything just yet but not wanting to dash Charmaine's hopes.

"I mean...," he said, "...is okay."

The pair smiled and hugged, before Oleg

turned to address A.J.

"Thank you, Mister A.J. You are good man."

"Don't mention it, Alex, and one more thing."

"What's that?"

"Call me 'Dad.'"

***

The Saints' trip out west to face the San Francisco 49ers was a landmark, not only because it rekindled the teams' heated NFC West rivalry that had been quashed by league realignment in 2000. Even more noteworthy, it marked Ron Beauchamp's first ride on the team plane since undergoing heart bypass surgery more than five years earlier.

Beauchamp had heretofore gone the John Madden route for traveling to away games, having invested $3.2 million in a customized RV that chauffered him over the nation's highways in high style. But with his recent financial crisis, he had begun shedding assets like a hot air balloon dropping weight to stay aloft.

His presence on the flight was met with the same reaction accorded a crying baby or business traveler with a whooping cough. Had Beauchamp chosen to ride the entire flight in the plane's undersized lavatory, he would not have been missed. His awkward attempt to serve as in-flight host and cheerleader only succeeded in setting everyone on edge as he moved from seat to seat, trying to offer words of wisdom and inspiration to each player.

Making matters worse, Beauchamp reeked of Bourbon, of which he'd partaken liberally to calm his nerves, against doctor's orders, of course. So as not to hear any guff from the team's medical staff, he'd conveniently banished them from the plane, forcing them to catch a commercial flight. His lone travel companion was Fielding, who remained in his seat at the front of the plane, running and re-running numbers while his boss made the rounds, dispensing trite maxims and unwanted advice.

Beauchamp had just emerged from the restroom at the rear of the plane when a pocket of turbulence sent him crashing into the seat next to Oleg in the very last row. Eyes closed, Oleg sat with a book open on seat-back tray-table in front of him and appeared to be meditating on the words. He did not acknowledge Beauchamp's presence until the pilot spoke over the P.A.

"Guys, we'll be going through a rough patch here for the next few minutes, and things might get a little bumpy," the pilot said. "Please remain seated and buckle your seatbelts until we give the all-clear. Thanks."

"Ahh, Christ," Beauchamp said, cinching his belt tight and gripping both armrests for support. "Here we go again."

Oleg opened his eyes and stared coldly at the man who signed his paychecks. "Is problem?"

"These damn airplanes make me more nervous than a priest in a whorehouse. But I'll be okay. Just as soon as we touch down in San Francisco. Yessiree."

Relaxing a bit, Beauchamp turned slightly in his chair to get chummy with Oleg. "You know, 'Leg, I don't believe we ever really spent much quality time together, you and I, especially after you callin' me a pig and all that."

Oleg remained silent, seeing that Beauchamp was prepared to do the talking for the both of them. Alcohol aside, Beauchamp felt his best in weeks because the L.A. consortium had resumed its interest in the Saints after their talks with the Minnesota Vikings fell through.

"Aw, hell, don't worry about it, son," Beauchamp said. "That was all in the past. Besides, if it wasn't for you, we wouldn't all be in this situation, now would we? Just when you think your luck's run out..." His voice trailed off, and he chuckled. "Can you keep a secret?"

Oleg shrugged but remained noncommittal. This did nothing to deter Beauchamp's eagerness to share information. He leaned close and lowered his voice. "Between you and me, Fielding and I have a meeting with the bigwigs from L.A. just as soon as we touch down."

"So then you are not going to make new deal with governor?" Oleg said. "I read in newspaper that she is assembling group to buy Saint."

Beauchamp burst into a fit of laughter. Oleg couldn't figure out what was so funny.

"Son, you just keep kicking footballs and let that fine sister of yours do your business for you. Because it's obvious you don't know thing one about making a good deal."

"I guess I do not understand."

Beauchamp leaned in again, this time so close that Oleg could smell the alcohol fumes. It was times like this when Ron Beauchamp got so full of himself, he had to let someone else in on his secret just to let them know how brilliant he was. Times like this when prudence went out the window. "You see, kid, by my calculations, the most Governor Fontenot and her crew would ever be able to come up with is about three hundred million. But that's chump change. Especially for those L.A. boys who want a new football team in Hollywood. By the time Fielding and I get through with them, this deal is gonna' make history."

"You should bring Minka with you," Oleg said. "She is real, how you say, ball-breaker."

Beauchamp laughed. "You have a point, but I think we'll be okay without her. With the product we got now, we could rightfully get $600 million. But I think we can hold out for seven."

Oleg frowned. "But then team will move?"

"Now wait a second. Don't get ahead of me here. What's so brilliant is that we'll be able to make the deal, pay down our debt, and have enough to invest in a new team."

"A new, New Orlyuns Saint?"

"Well, I don't know about that," Beauchamp said. "For starters, it could be a few years before the league allows another expansion. And then there's the matter of a piece of land I got now sittin' vacant over in Biloxi. Could put a nice stadium right on top of the ruins of Beau Maison Resort & Casino."

Oleg grew concerned. "But what will people in New Orlyuns do for football?"

"They'll still have Tulane...LSU."

"But I mean real team. Professional team."

"They'll get over it, I'm sure."

"But what about public money you have used? Money belongs to people. You owe something to them, yes? Is their money, is their team."

Beauchamp began to shake his head and sigh. "Son, I don't think you're understanding how capitalism works."

"That is not capitalism. Is thievery if you take people's money and give them nothing in return. You need to buy another team and keep Saint in New Orlyuns."

"That wouldn't be very practical," Beauchamp said. Although he found the challenge from Oleg maddening, underneath his glib exterior, pangs of guilt still gnawed away at him. And he knew that, should he sell and the team move, he'd all but have to pack up and leave New Orleans. Still, he reasoned, at least he'd do it with his Beau Maison empire intact and several hundred million dollars profit as lagniappe.

"Does not matter what is practical," Oleg said. "All that matters is what is right."

"Look, we could try and bring a team back to Nooawlins, but we'd still be fightin' the same battles all over again – the stadium, the local business community, the fan base."

"Would mean New Orlyuns have team, yes?"

"You just don't get it, do you?" Beauchamp said. "It's like my first wife said, the definition of crazy is doing the same thing over and over and expecting a different result."

"I do not think *you* get. Aristotle say, definition of crazy is seeking profit from all things."

"I beg your pawdon. How dare you question my motives, especially when you don't know me from Adam? One thing you need to understand is that this team's been cursed since day one, and we're still fightin' an uphill battle."

Oleg was unimpressed. "Even Moses had to walk through desert to get to Promised Land."

"Oh, you can lay off the sermon."

"Seems to me is something special about this team," Oleg said. "I think New Orlyuns Saint are blessed, not cursed."

"Ha! Yeah, you and the Pope."

Oleg smiled and tried to calm Beauchamp.

"Look, I have been skeptic, too. But is clear now. You cannot run from who you are. Team may have problem in past, but is only team New Orlyuns have. Is like family. Is part of city. Cannot toss aside like ex-wife and buy another one."

"Now you leave my personal life out of this," Beauchamp said, his anger mounting.

"Is not about winning and losing," Oleg said, his smile dissipating. His tone grew more insistent. "Is about the thrill of playing the game. About hope. Even if only hope for next season. If you move Saint, that hope is gone."

"I'm not running a charity here. This is a business. And if we keep losing money the way we been, we'll all come out on the losing end."

"No one will remember your money. They will remember that you move their team."

"I've never made decisons based on what other people think," Beauchamp said. "I base them on what's in my hawt."

"Well, then, if your heart decide to move Saint because of money, your heart is poison. Tell me this, if you die tomorrow, what will your legacy be?"

"I'll tell you what it won't be," Beauchamp said. "Some old fool sittin' in the poor house because of misplaced loyalty to a bunch of football fans who couldn't give a damn about..."

KAPOWW!

"What was that?" Beauchamp said.

"Was lightning from storm," Oleg said, pointing out the window.

"No, I mean...." Beauchamp lifted his hand to his chest and began struggling to breathe. He winced in pain and emitted a deep-pitched groan.

"Will be okay as soon as we get past storm."

"I can't breathe," Beauchamp said. "My heart. It hurts. Go...get...doctor."

"But doctor is not on plane."

"Well get somebody. HELLLP."

The commotion at the rear of the plane was just enough to catch the attention of several players through their iPods, and quickly, virtually the entire team had swarmed around Oleg and Beauchamp in spite of the captain's seatbelt warning.

"He's having a panic attack," Fielding said, "or heart attack...or something. Where's the doctor?"

"He ain't here," Dexter said.

"Well, somebody do something," Fielding said. "Who knows CPR? The Heimlich?"

"Not me," Robbie Gauthier said.

"This is too much for my nerves," Cedric said. "I can't look."

"Well what happens if he dies?" Dexter said. "That mean he won't move the team?"

"Possibly," Fielding said. Hearing the response, Dexter backed away, not wanting to leave New Orleans and risk seeing his fried chicken business languish in his absence.

"Somebody. Anybody, please help," Fielding said. Beauchamp was beginning to turn purple.

"Oleg, you're the faith healer. Touch him," Fielding said.

"I cannot help him."

"Just do something," Fielding said.

"Come on, Oleg," Kirk Wharton said, clutching a Bible. "God gave you a gift."

"Maybe God wants him dead," Oleg said.

"Come on, 'Leg," Oleg's teammates began shouting frantically.

"There is nothing I can do," Oleg said.

"Just do something," Fielding said.

Reluctantly, Oleg reached across the seat and placed a hand on Beauchamp's forehead and another on his heart. The limp body trembled underneath.

"Aren't you supposed to say something holy?" Fielding said.

"Now he's turning blue," Dexter said.

"Try giving him CPR," Fielding said.

"I told you," Oleg said, "is nothing I can..."

AHHHHHHHH!!

The plane hit a massive air pressure bubble, and, in the amount of time it takes to soil oneself, dropped a thousand feet in altitude, sending anyone who wasn't strapped in crashing against the ceiling of the fuselage and then tumbling back to the floor along the aisle.

But as quickly as it had begun, the plane leveled off and resumed a smooth cruising altitude, and the crisis had passed.

One by one, the men unpiled from each other like players on a goal-line stance. When they turned their attention back to Beauchamp, they saw his eyes fluttering open and his breathing return to normal. Slumped across his lap lay Oleg, unconscious.

***

"Ron, you sure you're feeling okay?" Fielding said, sitting next to Beauchamp in their seats at the front of the plane.

"I'm fine, I'm fine," Beauchamp said, appearing remarkably lucid considering what he'd just gone through. Oleg, meanwhile, remained at the plane's rear, having regained consciousness briefly, only to fall back into a deep slumber.

"You gave us quite a scare," Fielding said.

"Really, I'm okay," Beauchamp said. "I don't know what the hell that was, but it's definitely cleared up. It's like I feel ten pounds lighter."

"You sure? Should I call to reschedule with the L.A. consortium?"

"No need. Just cancel it."

"What?"

"Cancel it. I'm not going to sell."

"What do you mean you're not going to sell? You have to sell. Otherwise you're broke."

"At least not to them. I can't move the team."

"But, Ron, you have to move the team," Fielding said. "There's nobody in New Orleans in a position to buy it."

"Listen to me very closely," Beauchamp said. "I...cannot...move...this...team."

"Are you gonna' wait around for the governor to get her act together? We don't have time."

"Honestly, I don't know what I'm going to do," Beauchamp said, rubbing his forehead. "But I know I can't let the team move. Even if it ruins me financially."

"Ron, now let's not overreact here. You've had a stressful day."

"Look at me, Byron." Beauchamp leaned toward Fielding and stared deep into his eyes. "When all that commotion was going on, I saw something. I can't really explain it. I know it doesn't make sense. But I saw something."

"What?"

"Hell," Beauchamp said in a whisper.

"Hell?"

"I ain't kiddin'."

"Hell. Really." Fielding mulled the concept over in his mind. "Well, what did it look like?"

"Remember that Falcon game back in '80 when we lost in overtime?"

"I was in college then, but yeah, I remember."

"It was like that, only over and over and over. It was horrible. And you'll never guess the sumbitch who was doing play-by-play."

"Who?"

"Howard Cosell."

"Ooh, that does sound rough."

Beauchamp sat upright and turned toward the front of the plane. "We're canceling. End of discussion. Soon as we land, call and tell them."

"You got it, boss."

"Then find me a church. I gotta' go to confession."

***

With 1:30 to go in the fourth quarter and trailing the San Francisco 49ers, 17-14, Oleg pulled wide a 45-yard field goal attempt, marking his third miss of the day. It looked like the Saints' luck had finally run out.

Oleg returned to the bench, where he had spent the entire game, ravaged by severe nausea, dizziness, and frequent bouts of vomiting. It was all he could do to keep from curling up on the bench in the fetal position.

The game had been an epic defensive struggle highlighted by more than a dozen punts between the two teams. Plagued all day long by intermittent showers, swirling winds and damp, heavy air, neither offense had been able to mount a sustained drive, and the scoreboard reflected it.

Now, all the 49ers had to do was kill the clock in order to advance to the NFC Championship game against the New York Giants. But these were not the 49ers of old. No Joe Montana, no Jerry Rice, no Steve Young. And as tailback Rickey Washington fumbled the handoff from quarterback Ray Rodriguez on the third play of the drive, the Saints accepted an unlikely reprieve, pouncing on the loose ball at the 49er 42-yard-line with just under a minute remaining.

In two quick pass plays, Robbie Gauthier moved the team inside the 49er 20-yard-line. But rather than settle for a less-than-automatic field goal, Jake Radke went for the win. After a screen pass to Cedric put the ball at the 8, with time winding down, Robbie connected with Jordash Jones in the end zone on a perfectly executed fade route.

While the Saints' sideline went bezerk, the wine-sniffers at Candlestick Park, unaccustomed to being on the losing end of late-game heroics, fell into a silent stupor. Surely, their team could summon some of its former magic and pull off yet another miraculous victory. But the spirit of the "Comeback Kid" was nowhere to be found.

Oleg proceeded to squib the ensuing kickoff, which was about all he could do in light of his compromised physical state. After a pair of desperation heaves by Rodriguez, the Saints stormed the field to celebrate the dramatic comeback victory.

Everyone but Oleg, who remained on the bench, dry heaving into his helmet.

NFC Championship Round
10 Wins, 8 Losses

"You want to do *what*?"

"I want to go home," Oleg said, his voice echoing off the wood floors of his apartment. He lay on his mattress with an ice pack on his head, still reeling from the effects of the incident on the team plane. "As soon as season is over."

On the other end of the line, Minka shouted into her cell phone while riding in the back seat of a New York taxi. "Speak up, I can barely hear you. You want to do what?"

"I want to go to Warsaw, to visit Father."

"But what will you do? He has already said he does not want your money."

Oleg sighed, catching a glimpse of the fading afternoon light through the side window. "I will give him what he does want...my faith."

"Good," she said. "I see for once you make smart decision. Like television interview last week. I made couple of calls. Will be big in Europe. Maybe we get you endorsement deal."

"I did not make decision because it was smart. I made because it is what I feel. It is who I am. Is very clear now."

Despite the lingering physical infirmity, the incident had jolted Oleg's thought pattern like the reset button on a computer, and he was finally able to find the peace of mind that had eluded him for virtually all of his adult life. Ever since regaining consciousness on the flight to San Francisco, he knew it was time to "be who he is." Whatever his concerns, he was stronger working within his faith tradition than going it alone.

"Father will be pleased," Minka said.

"I am not doing for Father," Oleg said. "I am doing for myself."

"A-ha. You see, I *was* right."

"In a way, yes. But I am not entirely selfish. Maybe there are others like me."

"So you are going to become rabbi now?"

"No, no," Oleg said. "I will just kick ball. Use sport to bring people together. Christian. Jew. Muslim. Everyone."

Minka laughed. "Nothing is ever simple with you, Oleg. Can't you just kick ball?"

"But game is metaphor for life. Much more than winning or losing."

"Oleg, you are really something," Minka said, laughing again. "The way your mind works...you know, we are not that much different, you and I. Is just like in modeling..."

"To you everything is like modeling," Oleg said, smiling. He heard a strange beep on the line. "What was that?"

"Is other line," Minka said

"Then I will let you go. I know you are busy running business."

"No, it's okay," Minka said. "Is probably Fielding calling again."

"Fielding. Why is Fielding call you? Is my contract okay now that team is for sale?"

"Do not worry. Contract is fine. Fielding call because he think he is in love with me. He is like puppy. Always need attention. But he is cute, and very good with number. After someone buy New Orlyuns Saint, I may hire him to run my business. Figure he will come cheap."

***

"The Pope wants to do *what*?"

Ron Beauchamp practically wept in gratitude as Archbishop Boudreaux delivered the unexpected news. When Beauchamp originally called the Archbishop to set up a meeting to discuss the detailed process for saving his soul from eternal damnation, he had no idea it would lead to this.

"But is that legal?" Beauchamp said.

"Certainly," Boudreaux said. "The Vatican Bank has vast holdings spread across all seven continents. Stocks. Bonds. Real estate. Oil & gas. Gold. Jewels. Art. Just about anything you can think of. It's one of the most powerful financial institutions in the world. "

"And what about the league?"

"The league commissioner's a devout parish-
ioner of St. Patrick's in Manhattan. His Holiness
has already seen to it that there will be no
objections. Just name your price."

In his wildest dreams, Beauchamp never for a
moment imagined he would be in this position.
But amid his racing thoughts, his business
instincts kicked in, and he established his negotiating stance.

"Six-fifty."

The Archbishop chuckled. "Come now,
Ronald. The Pontiff reads the papers. He knows
of your business crisis..."

"Okay...six."

"And the many woes inflicted upon your
enterprise by Acts of God. After all, the next
hurricane season is only eight months away. I'd
think a man like you would want all the insurance he could get, including a little help from the
man upstairs."

Beauchamp sighed. He had never done
business with the Church before. These guys
were ruthless.

"Okay...three-fifty." He could practically hear
the Archbishop smiling, and Beauchamp knew he
was taking it up the rectory on the deal.

"That's getting there," Boudreaux said. "But
really, now, Ronald, we're talking about more

than just money here, aren't we? We're talking about your soul, your peace of mind. Is that truly, pardon the expression, your honest-to-God best price?"

Beauchamp turned to Fielding, who was, as usual, mulling over a spreadsheet in search of a misplaced comma or an extra million. "I must be losing my touch," he said. "First Fontenot, now this. If I can't outnegotiate a woman or a priest, I got no business in this business."

"What are you talking about?" Fielding said.

"Let me see that," he said, grabbing the spreadsheet from Fielding's desk and skimming the rows of numbers until he arrived at the bottom line. Reading aloud, Beauchamp muttered into the phone in a grudging tone. "Okay, here it is," he said to Boudreaux. "Two-hundred-ninety-six-million-four-hundred-eighteen-thousand-seven-hundred-twenty-four-dollars... and two cents. That's as low as I can go."

"Well then, Ronald, it looks like we have a deal," Boudreaux said. "We'll have a cashier's check to you by close of business tomorrow. Congratulations. I know that God will look favorably upon this gesture. Bless you, my son."

"Thank you, Your Eminence," Beauchamp said, hanging up the phone, still in shock.

"Ron, are you okay?" Fielding said, rushing to his side. "What the hell just happened?" He braced Beauchamp by the shoulders and looked into his eyes. Color slowly returned to the old man's cheeks and a smile spread across his face.

"The Pope..."

"What about the Pope?"

"He wants to buy the team."

"The Pope wants to buy the Saints," Fielding said, as though needing to speak the words himself to make sure he heard correctly.

"The Pope wants to buy the Saints," Beauchamp confirmed. "How could I not have seen it? Who better to own a team named the Saints than the Catholic Church?"

***

"The Pope wants to do *what*?"

Governor Fontenot screamed into the speaker phone inside her limo, as the car sped along I-10 just west of New Orleans.

"The Pope wants to buy the Saints," Jim Burton said, relaying the news from his office inside the Superdome. Beauchamp's aborted deal with the L.A. consortium had breathed new life into the governor's attempt to wrangle a group of investors to buy the team. At that very moment, Fontenot was on her way to town to make a last-ditch effort to keep the Saints from leaving.

"But what about separation of church and state?" Fontenot asked.

"They're buying the team from Beauchamp, not us," Burton said.

"And they'll keep the team in the Dome?"

"Not only that. But they'll invest thirty million in renovations, including a special box for when the Pope visits. Apparently, he's become quite enamored of American football."

"Okay, but just so long as we don't have any religious symbols. I mean, it's not like we can put a chapel in there. After all, the Superdome is a state building."

"Uh, Governor," Burton said, "technically, the entire team will be a religious symbol now that the Church owns them."

Fontenot thought this over for a second and shrugged. "Well...maybe nobody will notice. Hold on a second." Fontenot muted the phone and called out to her limo driver. "Otis, turn this thing around. We're heading back to the Capitol." She punched Burton back up on the line. "Okay, then, now that that's settled, it's time to get my re-election campaign underway."

***

"Up next on da line, we got John in Algiers," Lonnie B said. "What'cha say, John?"

In the weeks since the Saints began their record run, Lonnie B's nightly call-in show had soared into the top spot in New Orleans radio, and getting on the air with the irascible host was harder than getting a reservation at Emeril's on a Saturday night. But while Lonnie loved the renewed interest from fans, he had adopted a zero tolerance policy for stupid questions.

"Say Lonnie, I was wonderin' if ya might be able to help me out here," John said.

"Sure. What'cha need?"

"I was wonderin' if ya knew a good lawyer, 'cause I think I might hafta' sue somebody."

"John, what da hell's dis gotta' do wit' da Saints?" Lonnie said.

"Everything. Ya see, me and my cousin, Tre, bought a couple of dem bodybags at da Packer game, and he passed out, and I think he may have brain damage."

"What makes ya say dat?"

"Well, like, ever since, I don't know, he's just been real slow, I mean, slower than usual."

Lonnie lowered his forehead into his hands and groaned. "Tell me this, John, was you and him drinkin' at da game?"

"Well, yeah, but..."

"Heavily?"

The caller's tone turned boastful. "Aw come on, Lonnie, dis is Nooawlins. You know how we like our Dome foam."

"Sounds to me like both you squirrels are brain damaged. Next caller." Lonnie punched up another caller and drew a breath. "Next up, we got Diane from Gentilly. What'cha say, Diane?"

"Say Lonnie, I know you a man of God and all. Anyway, my brother told me dat when da Saints was flyin' to San Fran, Oleg and Beauchamp got into it, and den Oleg did an

exorcism on the greedy old bastard. And when he
came to, dat's when he decided to sell da team to
da Pope. It was a freakin' miracle."

"I tell you what, Diane, if you'da told me dat
eight weeks ago, I'da said you were crazy,"
Lonnie said. "But right about now, I'm willing to
believe just about anything. And if the Saints pull
this game out on Sunday against the Giants, who
knows...I might be signin' up for da seminary."

***

www.saintsforum.com

Posted by TigerMike 10:18 CT
Buying shares in the Saints
My wife does volunteer work for the Archdiocese, and
she heard that once the Vatican takes ownership of
the Saints, they're going to start a special tithing
package at church so that, if you put up enough
money, you can buy a share in the team, just like the
Green Bay Packers.

Posted by Brah 10:22 CT
Re: Buying shares in the Saints
Does that mean I gotta start going to church again?

Posted by TigerMike 10:23 CT
Re: Buying shares in the Saints
Nah, brah, you just gotta give them your money.

Posted by MawMaw 10:25 CT
Re: Buying shares in the Saints
But what if I'm not Catholic? That don't mean I gotta
convert, does it? I don't want nobody putting the
hard-sell on me just because I want to watch football.

Posted by Tookie 10:27 CT
Re: Buying shares in the Saints
Get real. The only thing they care about is money.

Posted by TigerMike 10:30 CT
Re: Buying shares in the Saints
Now come on, Tookie. I heard that if you own shares, you can get tickets at affordable prices. So, no, it's not all about money. It's about football.

Posted by Uncle Sam 10:32 CT
Re: Buying shares in the Saints
But if we all own the team, that's communism.

Posted by Ralude 10:33 CT
Re: Buying shares in the Saints
No it ain't. It's football-ism.

Posted by Uncle Sam 10:35 CT
Re: Buying shares in the Saints
Sounds to me like something they'd have in France.

Posted by Saint4Life 10:36 CT
Re: Buying shares in the Saints
Get real. Football is the most American thing going. Besides, you want football on Sundays or you wanna' watch freakin' ice skating?

Posted by Uncle Sam 10:37 CT
Re: Buying shares in the Saints
Good point. Now that the church owns the team, you think they'll start serving wine in the Dome?

***

Tim Anderson: Welcome back to Meadowlands Stadium. Let's take a look at today's action with a Double D's Game Summary, brought to

you by Double D's Fried Chicken. When you
want the biggest breasts in New Orleans, reach
for Double D's.

CoCo Pichon: This game has been everything that an NFC Championship game should
be. For the Saints, Robbie Gauthier has gone 22-
of-34 for 268 yards, two TDs and one interception. Cedric Wilson has 26 carries for 136 yards
and a touchdown, and the original Double D,
Dexter Douglass, has 8 catches for 114 yards
and a score.

Anderson: For the Giants, it's been virtually
a one-man show, CoCo, someone you know quite
well, your son and former Alabama standout,
second-year quarterback JoJo Pichon, who has
gone 38-of-52 for 406 yards and an NFC-record
five touchdown passes. Moments ago, the Giants
regained the lead as JoJo led them on a 58-yard
scoring drive in 2:38, capping it off with a 15-
yard strike, to give the Giants a 35-28 lead.

Pichon: Timmy, I can't even explain the
emotions I'm feeling right now. Pulling for the
Saints, pulling for my son. But it's been fun.

Anderson: Well, it's come down to this, after
the Saints just took their final timeout. With 10
seconds to play, they have to cover 68 yards and
score in order to keep their improbable season
alive. Oleg Adamowicz can't help them now. A
field goal won't do any good.

Pichon: I don't think they'd bother with it

anyway, the way Oleg's been kicking today.

Anderson: Yes, the Polish phenom has already missed two extra points on the day and seems a shell of his former self. It's been a pair of 2-point conversions that have kept them in it, with Gauthier completing laser strikes on both plays. He's really come into his own in the latter half of this season.

Pichon: It don't even look like Oleg knows what the score is on the Saints' sideline. He's sitting all alone at the end of the bench wth his legs crossed and his eyes closed like he's trying to levitate or something.

Anderson: Word is, he's been suffering from a mysterious flu bug for the last week, hasn't been the same, really, since the team's flight to San Francisco for last week's game. Well, regardless of what happens here today, if the Saints lose, it won't be on his shoulders.

Pichon: Here comes Gauthier to call the play.

Anderson: Every one of the 78,000 fans here in the Meadowlands is on his feet screaming for this final play. Gauthier in the shotgun, Dexter Douglass and Jordash Jones spread out left. Cedric Wilson in the backfield to protect.

Pichon: Get your rosary beads in hand.

Anderson: Gauthier takes the snap, drops back, looks, fires the ball underneath to Douglass at the 50, Douglass races toward the sidelines, stops, they've got the angle on him, oh, he laterals to Cedric who's racing upfield...

Pichon: It's like a rugby scrum.

Anderson: Wilson cuts across the field. He's at the Giants' 40, 35, 30...

Pichon: There's a guy gonna' catch him.

Anderson: They've got him wrapped up at the 28, he won't go down, they're gang tackling him now but Cedric's moving the pile.

Pichon: Wait, Tim, the ball just popped out.

Anderson: The ball's on the ground. Somebody's kicked it backwards.

Pichon: Here comes Gauthier from behind.

Anderson: Gauthier picks it up, turns, heaves it across the field.

Pichon: He's got Jordash all alone.

Anderson: Jones takes it in. He's at the 30. There's only one man between him and the end zone. He cuts left, gives the defender a shimmy.

Pichon: Man, he faked him out of his jock.

Anderson: Jones is at the 15, 10, 5, and, oh my God, do you believe it, do you believe it, Jordash Jones has scored with no time left on the clock. The Saints are mobbing him in the end zone, and Giant fans are stunned into silence.

Pichon: Amazing.

Anderson: The Saints convert on an unlikely 68-yard pass play that looked more like something you'd see on a sandlot. One of the most incredible plays I've ever seen, and it comes, no less, on the final play of the NFC Championship.

Unbelievable. Our score is now Giants 35, and the Saints 34.

Pichon: Oh, but look. The referees are gonna' review it upstairs in the video booth.

Anderson: Rightfully so. I'm not even sure of what I just saw. So the Saints will wait to see if they get the chance to tie the game.

Pichon: Oleg's up off the bench warming up. He's just got his head down like always, methodically going about his business, kicking the ball into the practice net.

Anderson: Before his mishaps today, Adamowicz was 27 of 27 on extra points since joining the team. But if you count the missed field goals in San Francisco, he's missed his last five kicks in a row.

Pichon: You think Radke would go for two here and just go for the win outright rather than playing for overtime?

Anderson: That kind of bold move wouldn't be out of character for Jake Radke. But I just don't think you can risk it, especially when you've got a guy like Oleg. Recent troubles aside, he's been the best kicker in the league the last ten weeks.

Pichon: Well, if he misses here, he's gonna' be walking back to New Orleans instead of riding on the team plane.

Anderson: I'm sure there'd be more than a few Giant fans who would offer to give him a ride should he need one. And here's referee Jerry Marklight with the ruling.

Referee: The ruling on the field is that it was a legal lateral pass. The player had advanced to the 28-yard-line when he threw it, and the ball did not cross that line in the air before the other player caught it and advanced it to the end zone. The touchdown is good.

Anderson: Oh my, well, we figured as much because Gauthier's desperation heave clearly did not travel forward. And the Giant fans are greeting the verdict with a chorus of boos.

Pichon: They're about as mad as a hungry gator at supper time. Somebody better get the referees a couple of bodyguards if the Saints pull this one out.

Anderson: Well, we'll know soon enough. The Saints are already lined up on the field. The Giants are scrambling into position.

Pichon: Looks like Radke's going to go with a kick. That's the right choice when you're the visiting team. Get this thing into overtime and see what happens.

Anderson: Gauthier is ready for the hold. Oleg is marking off his steps, lining up the kick. Gauthier begins calling out the signals. The snap is back. The hold is good. And the kick is...

Pichon: NOOOOOOOOOOOOOOOOOO!

Anderson: Oleg has pushed it right. The extra point is no good.

Pichon: NOOOOOOOOOOOOOOOOOO!

Anderson: This is the most incredible turn of events I've ever seen.

Pichon: NOOOOOOOOOOOOOOOOOO!

Anderson: The Giants win, 35-34, and they are going to advance to the Super Bowl. The Saints, however, are done for the season.

Pichon: Lord have mercy. I just about blew a gasket on that one. Who'da' thunk it?

Anderson: The Giants are mobbing the field in celebration, while the Saints' players have collapsed in anguish. At the 25-yard-line, Oleg Adamowicz has fallen to his knees and holds his helmet in his hands. No one is going near him.

Pichon: I gotta' tell you, Timmy. I'm tickled to death for my boy, JoJo. But that's no way to lose a ball game. I feel for the Saints' players and for all the fans listening out there. This one's a real heartbreaker.

Anderson: Let's not lose sight of what brought us here, though. The Saints made the playoffs for the first time in team history and came within an inch of the Super Bowl. Quite a lot to build on.

Pichon: My heart really goes out to Oleg Adamowicz right about now. He's obviously having some kind of physical problem, but it's an understatement to say that we all wouldn't be in this position today if it weren't for him.

Anderson: I'm sure that's little consolation

for Adamowicz. I can only imagine what's going
on inside his head at this moment.

***

Oleg remained hunched over on his knees,
grabbing his facemask, pounding his head into
the earth. Teammates and coaches passed by to
pat him on the back, one by one, offering encour-
agement. What they couldn't see was that,
underneath the helmet, Oleg was laughing. Not
the crazed cackle of a man on the brink. Rather,
the resigned laugh of one who'd now seen it all.

And why not? Just when he thought he had it
figured out, God threw him yet another curve-
ball. How could he not have seen it coming?

Throughout the team's championship run,
Oleg had remained remarkably even-keeled about
the bizarre events unfolding, while everyone
around him flew into hysterics. But finally, he'd
reached the limit, his capacity for reason exhausted. He realized that all he had left was faith.

Like a man walking through a foggy marsh
on a cool winter morning, Oleg had emerged on
the other side, and it all seemed so clear. He
rocked forward and rested his elbows on the
trampled turf, pounding the ground with his fists.
With each blow, his chest heaved and the waves
of laughter grew audible to anyone close at hand.

"Poddaje," he shouted. *I give up.* His words
rang out in rhythm with his fists.

"Poddaje. Poddaje. Poddaje."

His emotion swelled until the laughs turned to sobs. Only they were sobs of joy, because he finally understood that this moment, like all the countless others before, was part of a plan, no matter how convoluted it might seem. To know the answers, to remove questioning, doubt, uncertainty, would remove the mystery, the very purpose, of this grand experiment. Oleg saw that, in the end, life was a game, and there was only one rule, predicated on faith – not blind, unquestioning faith, but faith nonetheless.

Slowly, the energy drained from his fists, and he lay on the turf exhausted. Once his breathing slowed to a normal rate, he noticed that the pounding in his head had subsided, as did the nausea. He was going to be okay.

"Oleg, to jest w porzadku." A voice filtered in through the ear hole of Oleg's helmet. *It's okay. "Dostac w gorze." Get up.*

Oleg recognized the voice. He turned his head, lifted his torso and sat upright.

"Minka," he said.

"I told you I would be here," she said. She smiled, and her icy demeanor melted away. She helped him to his feet and pulled him in for a hug. "Is okay you miss kick. You are still hero of team. And everyone in Poland is cheering for you, after television show with your interview."

"Everyone but Father," Oleg said, dejected.

"Even Father," she said. "I made sure he

watch television for once in life."

Oleg tried to smile. "I do not believe you."

Minka chuckled. "You don't believe me? Ask him yourself."

"What do you mean?" Oleg said.

Minka stepped out of the way to reveal an ancient, stoop-shouldered man wearing an overcoat and fedora.

"Father!" Oleg said.

"Mój syn." My son.

The two men embraced, taking the first step toward resurrecting their relationship. Oleg saw in his father's eyes a look that he'd been searching for years to find, a look he'd all but given up hope of ever seeing. The rush of warmth flooding into his heart told him he was already home.

When they separated, Oleg noticed that Charmaine, clad in her black and gold Saintsations uniform, had joined them.

"Oh, Oleg, baby, I'm so sorry," she said.

"Is okay," he said, grabbing her hand and pointing her toward his father. "I would like you to meet my father."

Charmaine's eyes grew wide, and she reached out to shake the old man's hand.

"Oh, sir, it's a pleasure to meet you. Oleg's told me so much about..."

Before she could ramble on further, Oleg interrupted. "Charmaine, I have big question for you. I know is crazy time, but I want to ask."

Charmaine drew in a deep breath and braced herself for the question she'd been waiting all her life to hear.

"I want to ask if you will..."

"Yes, yes, I will, I will." She wrapped her arms around him and kissed him on the cheek.

"...come with me to visit Warsaw."

Charmaine pulled her hands back slightly and gripped Oleg by the shoulders. "Oh." The look of disappointment in her eyes was all too obvious. "I thought maybe..."

Oleg smiled and nodded. "Well, that too."

Charmaine engulfed him once again in a hug, as tears began to flow down her cheeks and visions of her wedding day danced in her mind.

***

Shortly after Oleg hooked the extra point, Ron Beauchamp shook hands with Jake Radke and made his way onto the field, moving from player to player to offer words of consolation.

Somewhere between Robbie Gauthier and Cedric Wilson, Beauchamp was overcome by the realization that his time as owner of the Saints was quickly coming to an end. And like a mourner at a jazz funeral, he began to dance the "Beauchamp Boogaloo" in celebration.

Roving the field for post-game interviews, CoCo Pichon took note of the spectacle and, in light of Beauchamp's recent travails, speculated on-air that the devastating loss had caused some kind of psychotic break in the famously mercurial team owner.

"Son, I've never felt better in my life," Beauchamp said in reply to Pichon's accusation. "We got nothing to cry about, no reason to hang our heads. We're workin' to win in Nooawlins."

"But this is your final game as owner of the New Orleans Saints," Pichon said.

Beauchamp's finger shot out in protest. "As majority owner," he said. "But once the Church takes over, I'm gettin' in line to buy a share just like everybody else. We'll *all* own this team."

"Yeahyouright, and I'll be right behind you," Pichon said. "I know there's gotta be a million things goin' through your head right now. Can you describe your feelings at this moment?"

Beauchamp paused a second and smiled.

"Pride, joy, a little sadness," Beauchamp said. "But mostly joy."

"Even though the Saints lost?" Pichon said.

"Look, we may have lost the game," Beauchamp said. "But if there's one thing I learned in all these years, it's that it ain't always about winning. It's the game itself that matters. And havin' a team here to play it. Our team.

"I want to thank the wonderful people in Nooawlins for supportin' this team all these years, and I want to say that, from now on, win or lose, we are *all* winners.

"Because from now on, we are *all* Saints."